The Revenge Tour:
Final Cut

Frank James IV

..ask him his dream, what does it mean, he wouldn't know. Can't be like the rest is the most he'll confess, but the time is running out and there's no happiness...

Curtis Mayfield – *Super Fly*

This is the first installment of a series I call, "The Revenge Tour." The Revenge Tour will be a series of tales about people who take matters of honor into their own hands. These stories will showcase people who either purposely, or indirectly, wronged someone, and wind up paying the price. In the future we will give other authors the opportunity to showcase their story telling skills on the Revenge Tour. Our first tale is called, Final Cut. So, sit back Dear Reader and enjoy the story of Calvin Hines and the satisfaction he indulged in. We open with Calvin standing in the woods looking at the stars over head with a shovel in his hand....

CHAPTER ONE
Revenge is a dish best served cold - Unknown

Calvin Hines grinned as he stood looking up at the stars. "You can see the stars clear in the sky from here. This is a good place my man. If you look over to the west, you can see the top of the Malco Drive in movie. See, I was looking out for you. You are in a great spot." Calvin shrugged and spun the shovel like a majorette spinning a baton singing, "They try so hard, but we run the yard!" He stood looking down at the spot for a few minutes. Calvin sighed, "Well, my man I must be going. I wish you well and remember I kept my word. You had, and still, have a chance." Calvin nodded and looked down at the freshly covered spot in the ground. He thought of tamping it down some more but decided that would not be fair and honorable. Calvin nodded and grinned as he headed back to his truck that was parked about half a mile away.

As he walked away Calvin found that he was feeling horny and may have to stop by the Diamond on his way home. Some head in the private dance area would be the perfect finishing touch to the night. Calvin was singing as he headed to the truck. The freshly covered spot seemed to bulge as if something were pushing from underground for a few seconds. Then the bulge settled and silence, except for the normal forest sounds resumed. By the time Calvin started his truck and drove off, the ground had settled and was fast becoming just another patch of ground in the forested area.

A few months earlier

Calvin was staring at his cell phone in wonder. Jack Davis, or Jackie as he was known to his friends, was telling him that he wanted Calvin to be the Assistant Director on his next film. Calvin was excited because his small video company Hines Film was barely making it. Calvin sometimes worked evenings as security on Beale Street to pay his bills. The chance to work with Jack was an opportunity Calvin could not pass up. Also, the film was going to be shot in Brazil. Calvin eagerly said he was in. Jack laughed and told him he would receive a small stipend of 3,000 dollars and a per diem of 20 dollars a day. Calvin knew this was fine with him because the US dollar usually was worth three to five of Brazilian money. Jack told Calvin that he needed to bring his camera and lighting equipment. Calvin didn't mind and agreed to bring whatever equipment Jack needed. Jack told him the dates and when to be at the airport. Calvin was excited and looked forward to getting on the plane.

Later when Calvin looked back in retrospect, he realized he should have seen the signs. Jack had promised to send him a contract detailing his job duties and pay. This never happened. Calvin was usually a shrewd businessman but, he threw all his business savvy away when dealing with Jack. In retrospect, Jack threw a lot away by how he dealt with Calvin. Calvin never did get his contract or paid for working on the movie. But let's not get a head of ourselves.

Calvin met Jack at the airport with his equipment. Jack had a lot of equipment also and both men wondered if they would be able to get the equipment into the country. They did. Jack had a connection in Rio who was going to serve as the producer on the movie in Rio. The guy's name was Kevin Fernandez. Kevin was from Rio and had been some sort of media star at one time. Kevin and Calvin hit it off right away. That was the one bright spot Calvin would say later that came out of the experience. When Calvin and Jack landed Kevin was waiting by luggage return grinning. Getting the equipment into the country was no problem because Kevin had connections at the airport that worked in customs.

Filming of the movie went smoothly. Kevin had hired another guy to be the production manager of the Rio side, Juan Atkins. Jack explained to Calvin his AD, assistant director, duties while letting Calvin know that he need not worry about doing any shooting or lighting. Jack told Calvin to focus on his AD duties. The director of photography was a female Jack knew from a film they had worked on before. Her name was Ellen Kincaid. Ellen was so laid back that Calvin found himself wondering if she cared about anything. Calvin felt this way until the first day of filming. Ellen turned out to be a stickler for details and good at what she did. Calvin found himself learning how to line up shots and angles from Ellen. Ellen was a bland woman as far as looks. When it came to camera and film knowledge she was on point. Calvin learned more from her in four weeks than a year in college. Jack was a great help to Calvin in learning what an AD's role encompassed. This was crucial since Calvin had never performed the role before. It was towards the end of the shoot where Calvin began to see Jack in a different light.

Jack had promised Calvin a 20 dollar a day per diem to eat and buy little things. Calvin wasn't worried about this part of the money. Calvin understood that Jack was an independent film maker and sometimes the budget ran tight. Calvin was looking at the big picture. This film would put Hines Production on the map. Until Jack got on the map, money was probably tight, so Calvin wasn't pressed about the per diem. The first week in Brazil Jack gave Calvin per diem for a week. Jack told Calvin that he could transfer the total amount of per diem sum for the entire shoot into Calvin's account, if he wanted the money. Calvin respectfully declined. Calvin was having a hard time eating and sleeping, so money to eat didn't mean much. Calvin didn't do any shopping, so he held on to the per diem money from the first week. It was during the second week of shooting that Jack began to borrow small amounts of cash from Calvin. This money was small sums to give to the van driver for fuel or buy something small for the set. Calvin was okay with this because he was dedicated to Jack's project. Also, Calvin was just giving Jack the per diem back. Jack didn't seem to understand Calvin's dedication or appreciate it. Maybe if he had things may have gone differently.

Calvin was from a minority neighborhood in Milwaukee. When Calvin turned 16, he moved to Detroit to live with his father. It was in Detroit during the Motor Cities heyday as the Murder Capitol of the World where Calvin became a man. Calvin grasped the concept of standing by your guys no matter what the odds. Calvin had been nurtured on gin and malt liquor beer in a city where love was a weakness that was often exploited. A place where your friends may number one, if you were lucky, and be named Smith and Wesson if you weren't. Calvin understood when someone was real, and when they were trying to give you a hand. In Calvin's mind Jack was giving him a hand or assist to get his name out there and jump start his video business. To Calvin this meant Jack deserved unquestioned loyalty.

On the other hand, Jack had some street in him, but not to the degree of Calvin. If Jack had similar upbringings, he would have understood that in Calvin he had a loyal soldier. A soldier who would go the wall with him. But, that kind of loyalty worked both ways. Loyalty on the streets could easily turn to hatred if the loyalty was not accepted and appreciated. Jack did not know this or understand this fact. Calvin did. To Calvin there was nothing worse than a friend betraying you or ignoring a friend's needs. Calvin would never turn his back on a friend who had been real with him. Calvin would not even consider committing the act of betraying a friend. Betrayal was not in Calvin's mental makeup.

Calvin worked hard for years to not see things the way he would as if he were on the West side of Detroit in the 90's. Calvin had come out of the trap that was the dope game and hustling to create a square life in Memphis. Calvin took pride in the fact that he wasn't doing time behind bars or enjoying a long nap in a coffin. But the things he learned, and core of his being was still Detroit made. So, when interactions or things Jack did began looking shady to Calvin, he ignored them and made himself not think like he was still in the streets. This led to small slights between the men that could have been addressed, stockpiling. Eventually Calvin's mind began to tell him that Jack had betrayed him. To reciprocate, Calvin naturally fell into his upbringing. The borrowing of the per diem was the foundation/beginning of Jack's betrayal in Calvin's mind.

When Jack asked to borrow Calvin's per diem the first time Calvin didn't think nothing of it. A few days later Jack gave him another week worth of per diem money. Calvin still wasn't sleeping or eating. Calvin just didn't seem to be able to rest or totally relax. Ellen noticed this and told Jack that she thought Calvin needed a rest. Jack waved her off but did ask Calvin if he was okay. Calvin told him yes, because even though he wasn't eating or sleeping regularly, he was learning a lot from working on the film. Plus, Calvin was a trooper and used to stay up for days at a time when he was hustling in Detroit. Calvin felt he could make the month of shooting with the amount of sleep and food he was getting. Jack didn't push the issue.

When Jack approached Calvin again to borrow his per diem, Calvin asked, "Man, when will I get my contract?" Calvin was joking, but serious about the contract. Jack got a peculiar look on his face and took the money Calvin was handing him. "You'll get it my man." Calvin smiled and thanked him. Jack started to tell Calvin he would get him his money back and Calvin waved him off, "Put it on my stipend." Jack chuckled and walked away. Calvin wasn't worried about money because there was an ATM in the hotel they were staying at. Before he left the USA Calvin had transferred some money into his traveling account. The sum was enough to purchase a plane ticket home, and then some, if things went bad in Rio. Calvin had also brought 1500 in cash with him just in case he fell in lust with some Brazilian females.

They finished filming on a Wednesday night. Jack had a conference area reserved at the hotel they were staying at, and the cast and crew had a wrap party. During the party Calvin snuck back to the room. For the first time since Calvin had been in Rio, he fell asleep and slept soundly. Calvin was woken up by someone knocking on the door. It was Jack in his briefs with two females behind him. Calvin looked at the women, then Jack, thinking, "Man, we in Rio and you fucking these two ugly women." Jack liked "thick" women. The two females with him that morning were BBWs, to say the least. For one fleeting instant, Calvin was worried that Jack was going to try to hook him up with one. Jack dispelled these thoughts by saying, "Man, let me borrow some money. I got to pay these two for last night." Jack looked lecherously at Calvin who worked hard to hide the disgust he felt. Calvin said "Okay," and shut the door on the trio. As Calvin went to get the money he said to the empty room, "This nigga supposed to be married. His wife must be shitty in bed to have him cheating on her with those two big ones." Calvin returned to the door and handed Jack the money. Jack looked at it while counting it, "I'll give it back to you later today. Oh, take the day off. Tomorrow, we have to make some media stops, but today go to the beach or rest." Calvin smiled and said, "Will do my man." Calvin shut the door and went to lay down and grab another hour or so of sleep. Before he nodded off, he smiled thinking, "I'll spend my day off at the Termas Monte Carlo." The thought made him fall asleep smiling.

If Jack didn't understand Calvin, then the same can be said about Calvin understanding Jack. Calvin didn't know that Jack had been the youngest child and only boy in a house full of sisters. Jack had four sisters and the closest one to him was seven years older than him. Jack was babied and coddled by his mother and sisters. Jack's father had left the family to go live with another woman when Jack was three years old. Sexuality in Jack's home was always blurred. For instance, it was nothing to Jack to wear panties until he was six years old when his mother's male friend found out. The male friend was outraged that Jack had on a pair of panties instead of underwear. Jack's mother was nonplussed and said, "All of his underwear was dirty. What is wrong with him wearing some panties until we wash?" The male friend had to turn away to keep from striking her while reminding himself that Jack wasn't his child. Needless to say, that was the last time Jack wore panties, until he was in college. In college Jack had a brief sexual identity crisis where he indulged with a fellow male student for a few weeks.

Because of Jack's upbringing he had some peculiar tendencies that are often connected to females. Calvin didn't know Jack had these tendencies. If Calvin had of known about these tendencies, he would have understood why Jack acted so emotional and petty at times. Also, Jack hated people who seemed like a part of the poplar crowd. Jack had never been popular at any level of school. Jack was extremely smart and got straight A's but was too clumsy to play sports. Jack was also too goofy looking to be a ladies' man. Jack got a lot of sex because he used his status as a film student, and later film director, to his benefit. There was never a shortage of foolish women who didn't see him but saw the camera. Jack liked Calvin and his work but, when he looked at Calvin, he saw the popular faction that never accepted him. Even with his minor success in independent film, Jack was still a nerd underneath. This underlying resentment of popular people assisted Jack on the path he took when dealing with Calvin. If Calvin had of known even one or two of these facts about Jack, he would have probably excused Jack's actions and felt pity on him. But Calvin didn't know these truths. Calvin didn't understand Jack and Jack didn't understand Calvin. With ignorance on the part of both men, the events played on until the conclusion.

The final few days in Rio was when Calvin began to see Jack in a light that was not positive. Since the filming was done Jack began to ignore, or act differently towards Calvin. Ellen left Rio to start another job in New York two days before Calvin and Jack left Rio. Calvin was kind of sad to see Ellen go because she was cool in his book. Ellen had always been good for a laugh, or to answer a question for Calvin. Jack was usually busy working with the other facets of the film to answer many questions or laugh. Jack had told Calvin that they were going to hit the local media circuit to promote the film the last few days in Rio. It was during these events that Calvin began to think that Jack just might be a bitch.

One of the first media stops Juan had set up was a radio interview with one of the top radio shows in Rio. The men went to the station and were met by the radio shows producer. Juan introduced Jack to the slim gawky looking man whose name was Philipe. Juan was about to introduce Calvin when Jack cut in, "This is my AD. He won't be in the interview." Philipe looked at Juan and Jack confused and then shrugged. Philipe then pointed to a couch outside the studio. "You can wait there." Philipe looked at Jack who nodded and the three men headed for the studio. Calvin smiled and took a seat. Part of his mind was saying, "What the hell was that about?" The other part of Calvin's mind was saying, "It's cool. Dude just stressed." Calvin nodded to himself, but said aloud to no one, "I didn't want to talk or say anything. I just wanted to be in the studio to listen." Calvin sat for 15 minutes and then stood and walked around the corner. He looked through the window into the studio. Calvin's eyes were drawn to the radio host. The host was a woman who had Calvin almost drooling she was so fine. Calvin said to no one, "That's why I'm out here. Dude must want to hit on old girl." Calvin couldn't help but feeling sick thinking of that fine woman with Jack. He shrugged and went back to the couch and waited. "Jack is cool. He my guy," Calvin said to the empty area. The seeds of doubt were beginning to take root in Calvin's head.

Juan and Jack came out of the studio with the Philipe who was shaking Jack's hand and smiling. Calvin stood and went by the men. Jack turned and grinned in Calvin's face, "It went well Bro." Calvin grinned, "I'm glad Bro. The movie will do well over here for sure." Juan finished up with the Philipe then came and slapped Jack on the back while looking at Calvin. "They love the movie concept and will push to make sure you get publicity from the station." Jack nodded grinning as Juan led him towards the elevator. Calvin hesitated and looked back at the studio. Jack said over his shoulder, "Come on Calvin. She too much woman for the likes of you." Juan laughed and Calvin smiled and followed the men to the elevator. A voice in his head was saying, "What the fuck is that supposed to mean?" But Calvin overruled the voice thinking, "I'm glad Jack's film is going to do well." Calvin had put the off-brand comment out of his mind by the time the elevator doors closed.

When the men left Rio the filming part of the project was finished. Jack was excited to go home and get the editing done. Calvin was happy for Jack because the filming had gone well, and Calvin truly thought the film would do good in Brazil. Calvin thought the concept about a man coming to Rio looking for sex, but finding Jesus instead was corny. Calvin was optimistic and felt the acting and international flavor would make the film sell. Calvin didn't think that the US market for the film was going to be good until it was accepted around the world. Calvin had told Jack that Brazilian money was money too.

Calvin had told Jack, "Make enough Brazilian money and it would translate to US dollars easy enough." Jack agreed. Once back in the states the relationship between the two men hit the skids, as they say.

Calvin was proud to be a part of an international film. With this in mind he told everyone about the film. Ironically, Jack began to become more negative in relation to Calvin because of these actions. Jack began to feel as if Calvin were trying to horn in on his work and glory. Calvin had posted on his companies Facebook page pictures of him working on the set in Rio. Calvin had also posted pictures of him with actors while wearing a shirt with his company logo on it. Jack hadn't thought anything about this when Calvin was taking the pictures and even encouraged it. Yet, when he saw the pictures back in the US, they didn't sit right with Jack. The final straw, in Jack's mind, came when he was meeting with an actress he was trying to cheat on his wife with. Jack had told the actress to meet him for coffee to discuss a possible role in the film. Of course there was no such role, but the actress didn't know this.

Jack met the actress at Starbucks on Union Avenue and began detailing what role she may play when she said, "That's Calvin's film. You worked on that in Rio. That film is done. What are you playing at Jack?" Jack was shocked. He stayed cool and smiled, "It is not Calvin's film, but mine. As far as playing at anything, I am not. There are some scenes I plan to add for the film that are in the US." The actress looked and nodded thinking. Jack took her thoughtful look as an okay. He began to talk about a bedroom scene when the actress cut him off. "If you want to fuck, it will cost you five hundred. That is my cost for bedroom scenes." Jack sat back sputtering as the actress smiled sweetly in his face. "How do you know Calvin?" Jack asked bitterly. The actress smiled wickedly, "Well enough to have already given up some free ass to be in a movie already finished." Jack took a gulp of his coffee, scalding his tongue. The actress laughed and began to rub his shoulder and arm. "Come on Jack. Calvin said you were going to be a big success. What's five hundred dollars to a big-time producer like you?" Jack was about to reply telling her to get the hell on, when he thought about the three grand he owed Calvin. "Nothing honey. Let's go get it on. We can discuss what role you may have in my next film." The actress smiled and Jack returned the smile.

Jack knew he owed Calvin three grand. "Well, we'll make that 2500," he thought smiling at the actress. Jack intended to take the five hundred and whatever tip he had to give this chick out of Calvin's stipend. Jack looked at the actresses inviting bosom and asked, "Is there a friend who may want to indulge?" The actress leaned over and nibbled Jack's ear engulfing him in her perfume and underneath that fragrance, her female aroma which was bringing blood to his penis. "Of course. For the right price," she whispered in his ear. Jack closed his eyes blurting out, "I got a couple grand to blow." "Then you have us both for the afternoon Jack," She bit his ear playfully and sat back while picking up her phone to contact the friend. Jack briefly thought, "Damn. What am I going to tell Calvin?" Jack knew his wife was his accountant for the film/ home budget and any funds removed would alert her. The one exception was the money Jack owed Calvin which was already put to the side. As he looked at the actress Jack thought, "Calvin can wait." Then Jack remembered that he didn't have a contract with Calvin. He had never gotten around to sending Calvin a contract. Technically Jack didn't owe Calvin anything. Jack smiled and said, "I look forward to the afternoon." The actress was smiling as she text her friend. Jack sipped his now moderately hot coffee and began thinking about how life was going to be grand once the film hit the theaters and the real money started coming in. All thoughts of paying Calvin had evaporated from his thoughts for good. Well, at least until later when it was waaaay too late.

Calvin was always glad to plug the upcoming film. Calvin knew a lot of people around the USA, and he made sure to reach out to all of them about the film. Calvin also used working on the film to promote his video business. Calvin decided to invest in some new editing software, and since Jack owed him three grand, Calvin decided to go Apple for the new computers. Calvin ordered a new Apple desktop with the hard drive capacity to handle the editing software and run a minor special effect software package. The cost was more than Calvin wanted to spend, 10,000, but he knew Jack owed him three thousand. Calvin ordered the computer and software assuming that Jack was going to pay him. Calvin used the money he kept stashed for emergencies to cover the shortfall from his equipment budget. The three grand from Jack would go straight into this fund to rebuild it. Calvin was about to get a hard dose of reality.

Calvin bought the editing equipment and it set up in his house. He had talked to Jack a week before the purchase and Jack told him his payment was coming. Calvin hadn't had a chance to think about Jack and the money in-depth because he was also bidding for a video job. The job was shooting a documentary about a film being made in Memphis dealing with the Civil Rights Movement of the 60's. Calvin had put a lot into the fact that he would be able to get the bid. One, because of his experience working with Jack. Two, one of the people doing the contracting for the film was a guy he knew really well, Pete Griffin. Pete also knew Jack. Pete had promised to get Calvin's bid into the right hands, and he did. Calvin went to The Memphis Film Authority and interviewed with the producers and director of the project. The meeting went well. At the end of the meeting the director and the two producers looked at each other and the director said, "It looks like we have found our guy for the documentary." The producers had nodded in agreement. One said, "If your references come through then we will contact you with a shooting date. Give us a week or so."

Calvin nodded and thanked the men. Calvin wasn't worried about his reference. One was Pete Griffin, and the other was Jack. There was no doubt in Calvin's mind that Jack wouldn't come through for him. Calvin called Jack on his way home and left a message telling him he would be getting a call, or email about him and the job opportunity. Calvin also shot Jack a text and email to let him know what was going on. Calvin was so confident in getting the contract that he cleared a few minor shoots from his schedule. The documentary was going to pay real good money and the publicity would put his name as they say, "out there." Calvin was wrong.

Jack had gotten the message from Calvin and at first was glad for him. Then he began to think he wasn't so sure about using his name to promote Calvin. Jack thought Calvin was cool and an okay guy, but he didn't know if he could handle doing a documentary. Jack sat behind his desk thinking about Calvin's performance on his film. True, Calvin had done everything Jack had asked of him. But that was because Jack was there to guide him. Could Calvin shoot and produce a documentary? Jack didn't know. He did know the people who were funding the film. Jack didn't want to risk his reputation by backing Calvin and then Calvin messed up. "No. No. I won't give him a recommendation. I won't bash him either. I won't say anything," Jack thought.

When the call from the director came, Jack didn't take it. When the email came from the producers, he ignored it. Jack listened to the messages, there were three of them, telling him that there was a time limit on when he could respond. Jack simply didn't respond. The fourth message was from one of the producers that knew Jack. The producer said, "Since he, Jack, wasn't responding they took his lack of response in the sense of Calvin was not a good fit. If they were wrong to let them know." Jack did no such thing. Jack simply pretended that Calvin, or the opportunity didn't exist. This also meant that Jack had an excuse to avoid Calvin, and this meant no payment. At least not in the way Jack thought.

While Jack was sabotaging his career, Calvin was flying high. The prospect of doing the documentary had Calvin on top of the world. He told his friend Paul Webb that he would be able to bring him on to assist on the project at a good wage. Paul was excited until Calvin told him what they were waiting on. "Man, I don't know," Paul had said when Calvin told him that the only thing needed was a reference from Jack. Calvin looked at Paul in confusion. Paul shook his head, "I don't know dude but, from what you say about how he played you on the money and acted funny...Can you trust him to give a good reference?" Calvin thought, then laughed. "Man, of course. Jack knows I can do this, no problem. Why wouldn't he plug me?" Paul thought then said, "Why won't he pay you? When was the last time you even talked to dude. I would have put someone else down. I'm not saying he won't come through...But." Paul didn't say any more and Calvin changed the subject. Later that evening Calvin had tried to call Jack, to no avail. Calvin shot him a text and didn't get an answer. Was Paul right? Was Jack playing him? Calvin had tried to shrug it off but couldn't. A few days later he got his answer. Jack had fucked him.

Two days later, Calvin was getting anxious about the project, so he called Pete. Pete was busy but said he'd call him back. Calvin puttered around with the new editing equipment and was amazed at some of the things the special effects software could do. His phone interrupted him from playing with the software. It was Pete. Pete had checked with the director before calling him back because he knew what Calvin was calling him about. "Calvin, they decided to go another way." Calvin was shocked to silence. Pete went on in a kind voice, "Yeah. Your references never came through. I did, but whoever you put down for the other one never answered the phone or emails. They assumed it was because you were not competent." Calvin was so quiet Pete asked, "Calvin, are

14

you there?" Calvin said false heartedly, "Of course dude. I was just listening. No big deal. I'll get the next one. Thanks Pete." Calvin ended the call. All Calvin could hear was Paul's voice, "Man, are you sure about dude?" Calvin called Jack, but once again got no answer. Jack's voice mail picked up after three rings. It was then that Calvin truly understood what type of dude he was dealing with. It was then that everything clicked into place for Calvin.

Jack had played him from the per diem, to the lack of a contract, to the fucked-up reference. Calvin went into the living room and sat on the couch. He then realized that hc had canceled his paying shoots for the next two months because of the anticipation of getting the documentary project. It also dawned on him that he had tapped into his emergency fund to get the equipment, that didn't have jobs to put to use. He laughed harshly at the part of his mind that said, "Jack will pay." The cold part of his mind knew Jack had no intention of paying him and that was why no contract ever came to Calvin. Calvin got up and came to a coldly rational decision. Jack was going to pay. Calvin began to laugh he said aloud, "Maybe his whole family will pay." Calvin was still laughing as he opened the refrigerator to get a beer.

CHAPTER TWO
"It's too late to pray when you have a gun in your mouth."
- R. Golden

The next day Calvin stopped by Jack's small office space in Midtown. Calvin didn't think Jack would be there, but he was. Calvin went into the building and up to the fourth floor. Calvin thought about the situation the previous night and decided to give Jack one last chance to make good. When he was about three doors away from Jack's office, the door opened, and Jack came out laughing with a little boy of around five. Calvin could tell by the oblong shape of the boy's head, and frail body he was Jack's son. The two were followed into the hall by a borderline obese female who was locking the door. Calvin figured this was the boy's mother, Jack's wife. Calvin noted Jack's tender looks at the boy and realized Jack loved this child. Calvin decided to file that away for later.

      Calvin spoke up as he walked towards the trio. "Hey little man! Jack, is this your son?" Jack froze for the fleetest moment then regained his composure and said, "Yeah. This is Jack Jr." He turned to the woman, "This is my loving wife, Sara." Calvin smiled at the boy who grabbed his father's leg and hid behind him. "Faggot," Calvin thought but he smiled sweetly and said, "High Ms.

Sara. It's a pleasure to meet you." Sara smiled and nodded while shuffling the oversized purse on her arm. Jack looked at Calvin and said, "What's up? What brings you over here?" "Nothing much Jack. I wanted to remind you that I was bidding for a job and used you as a reference." Jack smiled, "Calvin, you know I got you. When they call, I will let them know you are an excellent video production man." Calvin grinned, "Thanks Jack. I need the job just to keep the doors open." Jack waved him off good natured Sara and Jack Jr. went past Calvin towards the elevator. Jack Jr. was peering from the other side of his mother's meaty thigh as they walked past. Jack stopped by Calvin, "Man, don't worry. I got you on the reference and will send you a check for your stipend and the other money I owe you." Calvin nodded not trusting himself to speak. Jack clapped him on the shoulder again, "Come on before the elevator leaves us." Calvin asked, "Hey is there a bathroom up here?" Jack pointed back towards the office. "Down the hall on the left." Calvin said, "You head on out. I have to piss bad. I'll holler at you later Bro." Jack nodded and walked off.

Calvin headed to the bathroom and went in. He stood by the door with his eyes closed. Calvin had not wanted to ride in the elevator with Jack and his family because he didn't trust himself. Calvin could see himself grabbing that Jack Jr by his water baby head and either twisting his neck like a chicken or smashing his oversized head against the elevator panel. Calvin was breathing hard and had to calm himself. In Calvin's mind, Jack had just signed his own death warrant. Calvin was not an impatient fool. He wanted Jack to suffer, so a quick bullet in the head was too good. No. Jack was going to pay long and slow. Jack Jr would never experience puberty either. Calvin had decided to punish Jack by taking violent actions towards his son. The wife Sara? Well, Calvin wasn't a savage. Calvin didn't make war on women. Sara would live. The Jack's? All Calvin could see in their future was pain and a lot of tears. Calvin left out of the bathroom and went home to plot the demise of Jack and Junior.

Jack treated Sara and Jack Jr to a nice dinner at Folk's Folly. During the wait for the food while Junior was playing on his iPad Sara mentioned Calvin. "Calvin seems like a nice man. What did he want?" "Nothing much besides the reference he asked for," Jack replied while looking at the drink list. "Thats good. I thought he looked troubled about something, maybe money. But I realize we paid him a while back," Sara replied looking at Jack studiously. Jack didn't notice the look he was deciding on what type of martini he was going to have, chocolate or apple. "In cash, just like the man wanted," Jack told Sara deciding on the apple martini and putting the list down with a smile. Sara laughed, "Why these new business owners ask for cash is beyond me. We'll still report it to the IRS no matter what form of payment they choose. Bad business sense if you ask me." "Yeah, well we aim to please," Jack replied making eye contact with the waitress. Jack knew that even though Sara kept the books, the taxes were another item. That three thousand dollars would wind up being a write off. He grinned at Sara then the waitress as she came to the table. "Life was a beautiful thing," he thought as he began to order.

Calvin ran a few errands before going home. As he settled into his desk and relaxed thinking of Jack, a quick conclusion to his issues with the man came to him. Calvin kept a 38-caliber pistol that was, as they say, clean as they come. The pistol had been part of a stolen cache years ago. Calvin thought it had been at least ten years. The serial numbers would lead police to the stolen weapons in another state. Calvin highly doubted that the numbers would even get them that far. The theft had taken place in Chicago. Chicago police and ATF factions had other things to do than keep serial numbers for a stolen cache of weapons where 90 percent were recovered. Especially since the theft happened at least ten years ago. With this in mind Calvin knew he could simply go put two slugs into Jack's head and literally leave the gun right there and no one would be the wiser. Of course he wouldn't do the murder with the gun. But he could because the gun was so cold. Add in the fact that there was no tie to Calvin and Chicago, the act of getting away with the murder was highly probable. Yet, Calvin found himself frowning at the thought. No. Jack needed to suffer for his crimes. Calvin had already began thinking of Jack's actions as crimes towards him. With Calvin being judge, jury and executioner, the penalty was death. The conundrum was what type of death.

Calvin had ruled out quick death because Jack didn't deserve mercy. The type of death was what was puzzling Calvin. He stretched and turned on the Mac marveling at how smooth and quick it logged on. Calvin decided to take his time to plan and execute Jack. Calvin needed to find out all he could about Jack before he decided how to kill him and his son. To get some background information on Jack, Calvin logged onto Facebook. Most people put their entire life out on social media, and as Calvin found out, Jack was no different. By the time Calvin logged off Facebook two hours later a plan was forming in his mind. First, he would have to follow Jack to get Jack's daily routine down. This was no problem, because thanks to Jack, Calvin would be free for at least a few weeks, if not a month. Calvin sighed and said, "Steak one week. Ramen noodles the next. The life of a video producing ex-hustler." He laughed as he went into the kitchen.

As Calvin began rummaging through the refrigerator, he found himself warming to the thought of trailing and literally hunting Jack. The thought of punishing Jack for his transgressions brought energy to Calvin. As he began boiling some water for some cocoa, Calvin found himself anxious to begin the hunt/observations. "Tomorrow will be the start of a new game," Calvin thought as he grabbed the Swiss Miss Hot chocolate out of the cupboard.

****

In order to do what he planned to Jack; Calvin needed to know Jack's schedule. Since there were no video jobs scheduled Calvin had plenty of free time to gain this information. Calvin knew where Jack lived and started posting outside of Jack's house early in the morning to follow Jack when he first left home. Jack may have been about to blow up and become famous, but he hadn't just yet. Jack's neighborhood was the typical borderline area in Memphis. Jack lived on the East side of town on the borderline of where the white and more affluent residents of the city lived. It was not a slum area. Many people in the area were middle class African Americans. With this fact, Calvin did not have a problem parking a block away from Jack's house and pretending to either be smoking or arguing on the phone. Calvin only needed to do this when someone came outside their house and noticed him. The second day Calvin was watching the house a guy came up in his car and motioned for Calvin to roll his window down. Calvin did while pretending to be on the phone. "Hey man why you out here?" The guy asked. Calvin put on a troubled look, "Man this bitch driving me crazy! I was heading to work and had to pull over to get some shit right with her!" The guy laughed and said, "Man, I feel your pain," and started to roll his window up. "Don't let her drive you crazy man," the guy told Calvin as he rolled the window up and started to pull off. Calvin yelled, "I won't!" That was the only close call Calvin had.

By the third day Calvin had figured out the time Jack left home in the morning and would arrive a few minutes before he left. Calvin would begin tailing Jack's car around the corner from Jack's house. Calvin stayed about a half of a block behind Jack, even when they were on main streets. By Friday, Calvin had a rough idea of Jack's Monday through Thursday routine for heading to work and coming home. It was on Friday that Calvin observed the difference in Jack's routine that would enable him to get his payback.

Friday started out like any other. Calvin timed his arrival so that he was a block away when he saw Jack backing out of his driveway. Calvin slowed down and let Jack back out the driveway, then head off to work. Calvin followed about a block or so behind Jack's car. Calvin was thinking ahead and the possibility of going into a McDonalds that was a block from Jack's office. Calvin figured the office was where Jack was headed. He sat up behind the wheel when Jack turned and got onto the 240 West ramp. Calvin put all thoughts of hunger out of his head. This was a different thing, and he was excited. Following Jack to and from work had become boring, and frustrating to a point. It was frustrating because Calvin didn't see how he could get Jack before he got to his office. Snatching him up in his own driveway was out of the question. Maybe this new development would be something he could use to his benefit. Calvin turned onto 240 West and settled in to see where Jack was headed.

Calvin really became interested when Jack crossed into Arkansas. "Don't tell me Jack is a gambler." Calvin said to the empty car. If Jack was this would work well in his favor. Jack's car could sit for days at the casino, and no one would notice. It looked like Calvin's wish was going to be granted as Jack signaled and got off the highway at the casino exit. Calvin was confused as Jack bypassed the casino and headed towards the small business area off highway 40. He really became confused when Jack turned into one of the motels that lined the highway, Motel 8. "What the hell is he doing here?" Calvin wondered as he passed the entrance Jack turned into and drove down to the next entrance which was next to a Burger King. Calvin pulled into the lot.

By the time he turned around and made it back to the Motel 8 he noticed Jack's car was empty. "He must have gone into the place and got a room. Or went into a room." Calvin thought as he drove past Jack's car pretending not to look in. As Calvin started to drive around the building, he saw Jack coming out of the main entrance.

Jack was looking at some paper in his hand and holding what looked like a key. Calvin made the corner of the building and parked in the first space he could find. Calvin got out and hurried back to the corner of the building and peered around. Calvin knew he was taking a risk because if Jack had gotten into his car and drove towards the other end of the building he would ride right past Calvin. Calvin eased his head around the building and saw that Jack sitting in his car as if waiting. Calvin walked back around the corner and began putting two and two together. Jack at a hotel in Arkansas waiting in his car. Calvin laughed, "He is cheating on his wife. You cheating fuck." Calvin heard a car pulling into the lot on Jack's side and peered around the building to take another look.

Jack was getting out of the car and walking over to a car that had pulled into the space next to his car. A tall white woman was getting out. "Man, that is one tall chick," Calvin said in a low voice as he watched Jack meet the woman and hug her close. The woman was wearing a plaid mini skirt, red boots with high heels and a sweater top exposing a flat chiseled stomach. The skirt and dress were of good quality, but the woman's lack of breasts made the sex appeal of the outfit disappear. "I thought Jack liked them thick and big," Calvin thought as he watched the couple disengage from the hug. The woman was blonde and had a chiseled, almost manly jaw line. The woman grabbed Jack by the jaw and leaned over and gave him a passionate kiss, that Jack broke looking around. The woman laughed and said something Calvin couldn't make out. Jack grabbed her arm and began leading the woman to the motel room. The woman shook him off and stood with her hands on her hips. Jack turned looking around, when the woman said something that made Jack look down at her crotch area. Calvin almost blew his cover as he watched the scene. The woman had a bulge in the front of her dress. Jack licked his lips and waved her on as he went and opened the door to the room. The woman massaged the bulge seductively as she walked towards the room and

Jack. Calvin saw Jack go into the room followed by the woman and heard the door shut. Calvin almost passed out in shock and laughter. "That was a man! Dude gay as hell!" Calvin went to his car and jumped in. Calvin prayed that Jack had a rendezvous with the woman, or man, every week. If so, he knew where to grab Jack. Calvin started the car and drove over to Burger King. He figured it would be a while before Jack came out. He was right.

Jack was in the room all day until it was the time he would usually go home from the office. Calvin had waited expectantly for about two hours earlier in the day, before he decided to go to the casino. Calvin was taking a chance, but he figured that Jack used Fridays supposedly working hours to hook up with his tranny friend. If Jack was true to the form he showed in Rio, then he would be with the woman, or whatever for the whole day. Calvin was gambling that Jack pretended that he was working, and then go home like he would on a normal day. Calvin went to the casino and played the slots because he was feeling lucky. He lost 100 dollars and decided that Jack was really going to pay for this.

When he got back to the hotel at 2:45 pm, the lot had filled up with cars. Calvin found a spot on the other side of the building and waited. True to form, around 3:30 pm Jack came out of the room with the man or woman. Jack walked her to the car and kissed her. Calvin on a hunch ran back to his car and started it up. He made it to the edge of the building in time to see the other car waiting to pull into traffic. Jack was nowhere to be seen. Calvin figured he went back into the room. Calvin watched the car pull out of the lot and sped out from behind the building and used the exit/entrance on that end of the parking lot. Calvin pulled into traffic heading the same way the woman was going. Calvin knew where Jack was going, but wanted to know more about the woman Jack was messing around with. A little black mail before death may be profitable Calvin deduced.

The woman got onto 40 East and headed back to Memphis. Calvin followed closely because this person didn't know him, so there was no worry about being identified by them. The car got off on the 2nd street exit and headed towards Harbor Town. "Jack got him a money man," Calvin said to the empty car. Calvin followed the car and watched as it turned into Harbor Town. The car then drove down a side street and pulled into the driveway of one of the biggest houses in Harbor Town. Calvin drove past the car as it was pulling into the garage. Calvin shot a glance into the car and saw the wig was off and there was a plain looking white man in the car. Calvin drove down the block and then turned left and headed back towards the main road and out of Harbor Town. "I wonder who that white man is that Jack is sleeping with?" Calvin wondered as he crossed the bridge back into Memphis. What was important to Calvin was if Jack and the man hook ups were regular, as in every Friday? If so, Calvin knew how he could get Jack where he wanted him to be. An empty car in a low budget motel would not draw notice until a day or so passed, maybe longer. Calvin was upbeat as he headed home to formulate the next part of his plan. He now needed to come up with a way to get his hands on Jack Jr.

When Calvin got up the next day, Saturday, he decided to pop by Jack's house to see the lay of things on the weekend. Calvin only intended to drive by and maybe see the comings and goings of the family for future consideration. Calvin was in for a surprise when he got by Jack's house.

Calvin left home around 10:30 am planning on driving by Jack's house and maybe sitting around for 15 or 20 minutes. Calvin wanted to go work out, then go chill out the rest of the afternoon in Midtown. Calvin liked to go watch sports at the various bars in Midtown on Saturday. It was fun to talk trash with the sports fans in places like Local. If he stayed in Midtown until evening, he would check out the first set of whatever band that was playing at Lafayette's that evening. Calvin found plenty of female action on these weekends which was one reason his relationship with his ex-girlfriend, Helen, had come crashing down months ago. Calvin had truly liked Helen, but she was too needy. Well, not needy but wanted to be in his business. That was why they broke up. Helen had taken it upon herself to go through Calvin's phone. Calvin had set it down and went to the bathroom one evening at her house. When he came out the bathroom Helen was shaking her head looking at the screen of his phone. Needless to say, after several rude words being exchanged, Calvin was asked to leave the premises. Calvin had tried to reason with Helen, but to no avail. The last time he had talked to Helen had been two months ago, well before he went to Rio. That conversation was so brief that it may have only existed in Calvin's imagination.

Calvin had been down about the loss of Helen. In his mind the trade off in freedom was too great to lose much sleep over her. So, Calvin was back to hanging in Midtown and getting lucky with women most of the time. Calvin enjoyed white women and there were plenty of them in Midtown. If all else failed Calvin would hit a strip club and get some random stripper, or one he knew if they were working, to give his meat a lick and ride him till he was satisfied. The only problem with the strip club was it was expensive and quick. A whole night with a three or four level chick was a million times better than 15 minutes with a nine or ten level female in Calvin's book. This was especially true, after 10 or 12 beers added with a few shots of Jack Daniels. So, when Calvin arrived by Jack's house, he had no intention of being around for long. When he turned onto Jack's street, that changed.

Calvin turned onto the street Jack lived on a block from Jack's house. Even from that distance he could see something was up. There were people standing in the street looking at Jack's house. There was some kind of commotion going on. Calvin went half of a block up and then got out of his car. He was wearing a sweat suit with a hoodie top. Calvin threw the hood on then got out of the car. Before he shut the door, he grabbed the big black sunglasses he kept under the seat for when the sun was shining in his eyes while driving. Calvin put these on and headed towards Jack's house. He crossed the street so that he would be standing on the other side across from Jack's house. As Calvin neared the scene it became obvious what was going on. Jack and his wife were having a full-blown argument in the front yard.

Calvin couldn't help but grin as he walked up and melted into the growing crowd of about 6-10 people who were looking. Calvin asked a man in some Jordan sweats and t-shirt what was going on. The man never taking his eyes away from Jack and Sara who were arguing on the side of a car that Calvin assumed was Sara's said, "I guess the guy caught old girl cheating or something. They been yelling all morning. I guess she is trying to leave, but he won't let her." Calvin stood back wondering if he heard correct. "What the fuck? She was cheating? Oh, Jack you grimy devil," Calvin thought laughing quietly to himself. The man's assertion was proved right when Calvin heard Sara yell, "He is just a friend from college! Nothing happened or is going on Jack!" "Why the hell he texting you at 8:00 in the morning? Why were you getting up and checking the text in the bathroom? Why did you delete it?" Jack raged to Sara bringing a loud cry of, "Mommy!" From Jack Jr. who was in the car. Calvin thought, "What a bitch kid. And how would Sara react if she knew what your lips have been on Jackie baby?" This brought a laugh from Calvin which made the man and an obese African American woman who was talking on a cell phone turn and look at him with daggers in their eyes. Calvin somberly said, "You right this isn't a laughing matter." The two people turned back around nodding satisfactorily at his repentance.

Calvin watched as Jack blocked Sara from getting into the car. Sara was trying to run him over or around him to get to the car. "You are not going anywhere so get back into the house!" Jack was screaming. "Jack, I am leaving until you can get your mind in order. I'll be back tonight!" Sara yelled back. "No! Goddamn it! No!" It was after another few minutes of entertaining yelling and shoving that Calvin saw the patrol car heading down the block towards the commotion. The patrol car stopped and turned on the flashing lights. Jack saw this and tried to drag Sara into the house. Sara was twisting and pulling away from him, when she fell. You can imagine what happened next.

The police jumped out the car and before Jack could say, "Action!" He was on the ground with a knee in his back. Sara saw this and screamed, "Don't hurt him! Don't hurt him!" By this time Jack Jr. had gotten out of the car and was screaming incoherently at the top of his lungs. Calvin had seen enough. The obese woman had stopped talking on the cell phone and was now filming the comedy. Calvin figured it was time to move on. Calvin eased away from the crowd and walked down the block away from Jack's house and his car. Calvin walked then turned left at the corner and walked down a block. He then turned left again which had him heading back towards his car, just a block over. When he made the block and turned left again, he eventually came to the block before Jack's house. Calvin looked down the block and saw the crowd was still there, but he didn't see Jack or Sara. Calvin really didn't care what happened but, he had observed something that may come in handy. Jack was jealous and paranoid. Sara may be playing around on Jack. If Sara was then there may be an opening to acquire Jack Jr with little effort. As Calvin made a U-turn and headed to the gym his mind was thinking of all the possibilities that may unfold. In Calvin's mind there was no doubt that Jack and Jr were going to meet The Reaper. Calvin just had to put a plan together where he had a chance of getting away with the assist.

****

Calvin came up with a possible way to get a hold of Jack Jr early the next morning around 4am. Calvin was using his tongue to bring Samantha to an explosive orgasm. Samantha was a Tennessee Volunteer fan and had been in Local the previous day with some friends. Calvin had come in and began teasing the Volunteer fans in Local good natured about how they would never be any good in basketball. The Vols were on playing Vanderbilt in a conference game. There were a few Vandy fans, but the majority of the crowd was going for the Vols. Samantha had been vocal in her rebuttals to Calvin's jibes about the football program at Tennessee hadn't been any good since Peyton Manning left. Calvin knew mentioning Manning would rile Tennessee fans. Manning was the closest thing to a god in Tennessee that a man could come to without dying. Well, least in Knoxville and surrounding areas. When Tennessee won easily Calvin bought Samantha and her friends a round of beers to concede defeat.

Calvin hadn't thought anything about the joking or the beers because the next game was Duke against Indiana. Calvin spotted a few Duke fans and began to heckle them. Calvin heckled everyone. The staff at Local knew Calvin and let him do this. Calvin spent good money and always ribbed people in a respectful manner. Plus, Calvin tipped well. When it came to Duke though, Calvin laid it on the Duke fans. Calvin had a special hate for Duke. The image of good white boys and Uncle Toms just seemed to fit the Duke basketball image in Calvin's mind. It was in the midst of saying Coach K wore a toupee that Samantha came and sat down at the table he was sitting at. Calvin looked at her and asked, "Are you here to gloat?" Samantha said, "No. My friends left, and I wanted to stick around. Mind if I join you?" Calvin looked at Samantha, quickly taking in the pudge around her middle, bland hair, plain face and thought, "Yeah. I'll fuck her." "Sure. Have a seat and we'll watch Dookie get lit up!" He said the last loudly so that the Duke fans heard. One flipped him the bird making Calvin laugh while saying, "I'll pass. Christian Laettner may take you up though. I heard he likes it rough." This made the people in the area they were sitting at burst into laughter. The Duke fans even chuckled shaking their heads. Calvin waved a waitress over, "Send them a round of Bud Lights and bring my friend here one also." "Samantha. My name is Samantha," she said." Calvin looked at her and took a swig of beer, "Calvin. Pleased to meet you." They smiled at each other, and Calvin nodded to the television, "I'd better joke fast. It looks like Duke is about to run off with Indiana." Samantha looked at the television and said, "Yeah. But the game just began. Let's wait and see how it goes." Calvin looked at her and nodded, "Indeed let us." He winked at Samantha bringing a blush to her face. Calvin turned to the television, "Yeah. I'll be fucking this tonight," he thought.

It was during Calvin exercising his tongue that the idea of how to get Jack Jr away from Sara and into oblivion came to him. Calvin and Samantha had hung around Local watching the Duke game and the late-night Memphis game. Calvin and Samantha had both imbibed a good number of beers. Calvin worried that Samantha would get too drunk and suggested she slow down. "I know my limit, Calvin. As you probably guessed, I went to UT. Trust me. Beer was often used instead of water to quench thirst," Samantha replied with a smile and continued, "I'll still be able to drive home and perform any duties, or services I am required to do with whoever." Calvin looked at her and took a swig of beer and turned to the television. They had gone over to Lafayette's and caught the first set of the band playing that night. Both Calvin and Samantha were pleasantly buzzing by then. Calvin had suggested they grab something to eat at I-Hop or some other place in the area. Samantha had told him, "I have a frozen pizza in my freezer that will cut your hunger better than any restaurant can." Calvin had gotten up and said, "Frozen pizza it is." They left after paying the tab.

Samantha had the television on in her bedroom and *Revolver* was playing while Calvin was teasing Samantha's sex organs with his tongue. Calvin wasn't listening to the

29

movie. As he licked tenderly, he raised his head to get a breath and he saw the screen. It was the scene where the men used sleeping gas to put some criminals to sleep while they robbed them. Calvin froze. "That's it! If I can find a way to slip her some knockout pills then I'll have the time needed," he said in a low voice. Samantha noticed the break in action and gasped, "Don't stop! I'm almost there! Please keep going! I'll suck you dry!" Calvin smiled and resumed the task. Samantha said she'd suck him dry, but he doubted it. Calvin had a lot of juice, and it may take some doing to suck him dry. He was sure going to let her try though. While flicking his tongue in Samantha's delicate spots, a plan began to form. He attacked Samantha's pride and joy with gusto as he thought about the coming together of his plans for the two Jacks. As Samantha gripped his head while moaning loudly Calvin's mind was rejoicing in the realization of Jack and son's journey to the Here After.

CHAPTER THREE

"Grabbed that thang from under the seat, punched it his
mouth tried to break his front teeth!" – Action - JT Money

On his way home from Samantha's place later that Sunday
morning, Calvin decided to ride by Jack's house. As he
drove by, he noticed the car was still there where it had
been yesterday. As Calvin made the block and came
around for another pass he wondered if Jack was home, or
did he get locked up. Calvin was leaning towards locked
up, because when police came for domestic violence,
someone went to jail. In the USA the person headed to jail
was usually the man. Calvin turned and drove back by the
house and saw Jack Jr come out and run to the car. As
Calvin passed, he looked into the rear-view mirror and saw
Sara coming out. Calvin wondered if Jack was facing
charges, or did they just take him and hold him for 24
hours. From the brief glance Calvin saw of Sara's face he
tended to think that Jack was in jail and was either getting
out or would get out later today. Calvin wondered if Jack
would be home for work on Monday, and then started
laughing. "Don't worry Jack. If the trial is a few months
away, you don't have anything to worry about. I'll see to
that my man." Calvin was smiling as he headed home to
shower and grab something to eat. He needed to do some

research on knock out pills and tonics. He had a plan to get both Jack and Junior. The one thing he needed was for Jack to meet his "girl" Friday.

What Calvin didn't know was what was going on in Sara's mind. If Calvin had of known he may have saved some brain power. As Sara pulled out of the driveway after putting Jack Jr in his car seat her mind was not on getting Jack out of jail. Jack would be released sometime that afternoon, so there was no need to go get him out. She would have to pick him up, but not bail him out. Which was good for Jack, because Sara was beginning to think that she would not bail Jack out. She reflected on the argument that the two of them had the day before. Sara figured it was one that had been brewing for over a year. Jack was correct in assuming that she was texting a man, but wrong in his reasons for this. The man who was texting her was one she had hired a few weeks before. Larry Allen was his name and private investigation was his game. Sara thought back on what had led her to hire Larry in the first place.

Sara's thoughts were interrupted by Jack Jr singing along with some game he was playing on his iPad. "Shut up! Shut up!" She hollered into the back seat glaring through the rear-view mirror. Jack Jr promptly quieted down, and tears began forming in his eyes. "Don't start all that crying either! Damn boy you are one soft ass bitch like your gay ass daddy!" Sara was shocked with herself from saying the words aloud. Yet, she felt relieved by saying them. Jack Jr began sobbing silently to himself. Sara looked at him in the rearview and found herself looking at the child with disgust. The tears and shape of his head, along with his features reminded her of Jack. Jack was the last person she wanted to be reminded of. Sara cut on the radio and turned the volume up, ignoring the fact that the back speakers were right by Jack Jr's head. Sara's mind drifted back in time while the radio aired an advertisement about Viagra.

About a month ago Sara was the happiest wife in Memphis. Jack was her husband, and he was about to finish up his third independent film. This film was going to land the contract with one of the big studios that had been talking with Jack since his last film had done well on the independent film circuit. The trouble began a week before Jack was scheduled to come home from Rio. Sara had gone down to the office to double check the budget, and make sure there was still money left after the filming to get the editing done. Usually, Sara did her work at her desk on her laptop that sat outside of the inner office. The inner office was simply a desk behind a partition where Jack worked. For some reason, on that day she decided to use Jack's desktop which meant that she was working at his desk. Sara never used Jack's desk or machine because there was no need to. The laptop she used for the books and emailing clients was more powerful and faster. Maybe it was the fact that she missed Jack and simply wanted to sit in his chair. Whatever the reason, Sara made the choice and after she logged into Jack's machine, she wished she would have stayed home.

As Sara settled into Jack's chair she logged onto the desktop. The picture of her, Jack and Jack Jr came up as the other app icons loaded. Sara felt intense love for Jack as she looked at the picture. "Well, let's get to work," she said to the empty office. Sara pulled up the spread sheets and began looking over the figures on it and comparing them to the latest numbers Jack had sent from Rio dealing with costs. Jack had planned for everything and put money up to hold in reserve for emergencies. From what Sara was getting from the numbers, the emergency money would not be needed. According to the program and her calculations the film was coming in under budget. Sara knew Jack would be pleased with this because the extra money could go towards promotions along with editing. Sara put the latest numbers from Jack into the spread sheet and sat back relaxing.

Sara got on Google and began searching for houses in Collierville. When the money came in Jack had always told her that he would relocate the family to an affluent area so Jack Jr would be able to see more than the ghetto when he walked around the block. While on Google, Sara saw that the search engine was open under Jack's name. Being nosy she clicked on the mail setting. Sara knew Jack's business email login, had for years, but could never get access to his Gmail account. Even though Sara knew she was alone she found herself looking around the office. Part of Sara's mind said, "Girl why are you looking into his personal email? If you open one, he will know someone has been in his account." A louder more persuasive part of Sara's mind said, "Just check the ones that are open. Or simply scan his email list. You just checking on your husband, so there is no problem." Sara followed the latter mindset and began looking at the listings of emails Jack had gotten.

Sara saw that many of the emails were for products or services dealing with film making. A few were from old friends of Jack's from college or other films. Sara went through the sent emails also checking to see what was sent out by Jack and to who. For thoroughness, Sara checked the spam file. After performing this last task, and beginning to feel foolish, she went back to the inbox. As she was about to leave the email account, she remembered to look at any folders. Sara's mother had always told her to be thorough in any task when she was young and would half do a chore. There was only one folder labeled with the word, EYES. Sara looked at the name and shrugged clicking on the folder. There were about twenty emails from different sources. All the emails had the same subject line: EYES. Sara clicked the first email and wished she had put out her own eyes.

The email was blank but there were several pictures attached. Sara clicked one and avoided throwing up on the keyboard by the slimmest margin. She grabbed the garbage can next to the desk and threw up her Danish and coffee from that morning. Sara had a few dry heaves before she could gain control of her body. With water running out of her mouth and eyes she fumbled for the Kleenex on the desk. As she did her eyes glanced at the screen which led to a few more dry heaves. As Sara sat back and wiped her eyes and mouth, she looked at the pictures in shock. The pictures were of her husband in an all-male orgy, no gang bang. And from what Sara could see Jack was the one getting banged. More insulting was the fact all the other men were white.

By the time Sara finished looking at all the email attachments, she was beyond sick. A part of her mind laughed at her saying, "See! That's what happens when you look in people's private emails." The pictures were all of a younger version of Jack, and the dates on the emails were years past. The last one was three years old. Sara first thought these were some form of black mail, but one of the older emails had nixed these thoughts. The email was from one of Jack's college friends that she had met a year or so ago, that had come into town for business. Sara had recognized the guy in some of the pictures. She also realized that these pictures were from the same two events. In some Jack was getting it. Others Jack was giving. In all it seemed as if everyone was having a great time. Sara remembered something Jack had once said after they were married, "I don't judge people for their sexual orientation. Anybody can get fucked." This statement had made both of them laugh and Sara had put the incident out of her mind. Until now. How could she ever look at him again? Even if this was his college days, he was gay. Sara logged off the computer after swearing she would never log back in. She broke this oath less than 24 hours later.

Sara left the office that day and drove to the first Catholic Church she could think of downtown. Sara was not Catholic but knew from movies that you could go into the confessional and talk to someone. Well, that is what she hoped. Sara's hopes were not unfounded. Sara went into the church and sat in a pew looking at the stain glassed windows depicting Jesus with a lamb. Sara found herself looking at this image and thinking how much Jesus looked like the white boys who had been in the pictures with Jack. Sara got up and went to one of the booths on the side and looked in. There was an old white woman sitting in the pew who said, "Go on in young lady. Don't be afraid God loves you." Sara looked at the old woman whose clothes looked expensive, but whose complexion resembled a dead body and replied, "Thanks. Thanks, I will." Sara went into the booth and closed the door.

Sara left the church 30 minutes later feeling better about the situation. The priest had listened to her story with patience. He asked probing questions about her life and love for Jack. The priest even asked her about her feelings for Jack Jr. Once she was finished. The priest said, "You are not Catholic, but still a child of God. Sister put the past behind you. What Jack did in college means nothing to his life with you. Those pictures were from a time past. Leave them in the past. The emails were from years gone by from people Jack may not even keep in contact with. You have a wonderful child and the potential to have a nice life with Jack. Don't let the past ruin your present and possibly your future. Be blessed my child." With that the little window closed. Sara understood that she had been dismissed. When she stepped out of the confessional the old woman was gone. Sara looked around for the priest, but only saw a man in workman's clothes kneeling and mumbling something by the altar. Sara paused as she walked towards the exit. She wanted to thank the priest, whoever he was, for the advice. But all she saw was a nun lighting some candles in a corner across the room. With a shrug Sara left the church. The advice was great advice and lasted in Sara's mind for all of three hours. The next day Sara was back at the office. She had to know if the people who had sent Jack the pictures were in Memphis.

Sara found herself back at Jack's desk in his email the next day. She only wanted to get the names of the people who sent the emails to check if they were in Memphis. The emails came from three men: Kyle Long, Fred Hart and Jay Thompson. Sara used Google to look the men up. Kyle and Fred did not show up in Memphis. Jay did. When Sara clicked on images, she found plenty of pictures of Jay. There was no doubt that Jay was one of the men in the pictures. Sara also found out that Jay was probably a millionaire. The reason Sara felt that way was because of the articles she read about him. Jay was one of the architects who designed the Hyatt Centric Hotel and other relatively new buildings around Memphis and Nashville. There were pictures of Jay with the mayor of Memphis and the owner of the Grizzlies. Sara wondered if Jay had financed Jack's last movie. At one point at the beginning of the project, Jack was stressing over funds. Then in the next week, or so, he claimed to have the money and more. Sara decided to find out if Jay was Jack's benefactor. She typed in private investigator in Memphis on Google. She scanned through the listing and clicked on Larry Allen Investigations. All thoughts of the advice the priest had given her was gone. Sara needed to know if Jack was business partners and still having fun with his buddy Jay.

Later that day Sara met Larry at his office in Midtown. Larry had listened and agreed to get some basic information for Sara. The cost would be 1200 dollars, expenses included. Sara had always kept a bank account that Jack didn't know about. Her father had given her 10,000 dollars as a wedding present. Her father had told Sara this was her get out of jail free money. He told her to put this into an account or shoebox and never tell Jack. This was the money to use if she wanted to leave Jack and needed some startup funds. Sara took this advice to heart. So, when Larry told her 1200, she didn't blink an eye.

Sara got the call from Larry a week after Jack had come back from Rio. Sara had taken the call when Jack was out of the office. Larry had told her that Jay was one of the sources of funding for the movie. Jay had a maid who liked drinking Chivas Regal scotch and hanging at the bar in the Peabody Hotel after work. This maid had identified a picture of Jack as being the man who had come by the house in Harbor Town often for the past year. This maid had observed Jay write out Jack two checks for unknown amounts. The maid did say that when Jay handed one of the checks to Jack, Jack had grinned and said, "Jay this is enough for us to make a smash hit! Plus, you remembered to make it out to me." Sara had asked did Jack sleep with him for the money. Larry had answered, "The maid didn't say or even hint that such things took place. Maybe Jack just hit an old college buddy up for a loan and the buddy came through for him." Sara had nodded while holding the phone. Yet, those pictures roiled in her gut. "Thanks Larry. Can you follow him for a few weeks, just to be sure?" Larry paused, "If you want me to, I can tail him for a few weeks. It won't be cheap; 200 a day and you pay expenses up to 75 dollars." Larry figured this number would be too high and Sara would balk and let this issue rest. Larry was shocked when Sara responded, "Do I need to pay you now?" Larry regained his composure, "No. I'll bill you when the job is done. I'll contact you if I run across anything sooner."

Sara came back to the present as she turned onto 240 West and headed to Midtown. It had been Larry's text that set Jack off. Sara couldn't tell Jack about Larry until she was sure there was nothing going on. For a time, Sara guessed that Larry had found nothing because she had heard nothing. Friday evening was when things had changed. Larry called her while she was picking up Jack Jr from day-care Friday afternoon. She hadn't been able to take the call because the manager of the day care, Ms. Price, had told her Jack Jr had been in a fight. By the time she remembered Larry's call she was home, and Jack was there. Jack took the family to dinner at Houston's and was in a good mood the entire evening. Sara and Jack made great love later that night. Sara had to admit that if Jack was gay, it helped his stamina.

It was Saturday morning when Larry text her. Sara found this odd because Larry didn't leave messages to avoid a trail. The text was simple, call me ASAP. Sara was responding to the text when Jack tried to bust into the bathroom. All she had time to do was send a text saying: I will, do not contact me. Then she deleted both the text and the one Larry sent just as Jack damn near tore the door down. Now as she turned off the highway Sara wondered if what she had done was worth it. Was paying Larry the money and even opening the emails worth it? As Sara drove the last few miles to Larry's office, she had to admit that she didn't know.

By the time Sara parked the car Jack Jr was sniffling to himself. Sara looked at him and felt a pang of sorrow for her actions. She said turning around, "Hey. Sorry I yelled at you. We'll get some Chik-fil-A after we leave here." Jack Jr smiled and began wiping his face. Sara looked at the building and for a minute thought about leaving Jack Jr outside but ignored the thought. Sara got Jack Jr out of the car seat while handing him his iPad. The two walked into the building. Larry's office was on the second floor. Jack Jr asked, "Where are we going Mommy? To get Daddy?" "No. I have to pick up some paperwork for the office. It won't take long," she said not stopping or looking at him.

Larry was waiting in the small office that was nothing more than a desk and two chairs. Larry looked at Jack Jr then at Sara. "Jack put your earbuds in and listen to your song," Sara told the boy. The boy looked at the man, then his mother and nodded. Jack Jr sat in one of the chairs while Sara took the other. Once the two adults were sure the boy was listening to whatever song he liked Larry spoke. "I followed your husband Friday to West Memphis to the Motel 8. There he was met by what I thought was a blonde female who, was in actuality Jay Thompson in drag. They stayed in the motel room from around 9:30 am to 3:30 pm." Larry pulled a manilla envelop out of the desk and put it on the desktop. "Here are pictures of the two going in and leaving." Sara looked at the envelope. Part of her mind was screaming, "Don't look. Just take the envelope and burn it." Instead, her hands went to the envelope and opened it.

Inside were 10 glossy pictures of Jack and what appeared to be a woman outside a sleazy motel. On one Jack was leading the woman. One was of Jack kissing the woman. One was of the woman standing showing off a bugle in her crotch area. Sara thrust the pictures back into the envelope and looked down at Jack Jr who was eyeing his iPad. Larry watched Sara and saw the look of contempt, almost hatred, pass across the woman's face as she stared at the boy. He spoke up, "The negatives are in there also. Please do not attempt to black mail anyone Sara." Sara looked away from Jack Jr and laughed harshly, "Don't worry I have your money without stooping to crime." Larry nodded and stood up, "Good. When can I expect payment?" Sara looked at the man and pulled out a check. She had made it out before she left home, "Here you go. This should cover your fees and expenses." Sara stood and sat the check on the desk while tugging Jack Jr to his feet and said, "I thank you for a job well done. I hope to never have to see you or use your services again." Larry nodded not looking at the check, "As is your prerogative Sara. Have a great day." Larry extended his hand and Sara shook it briefly and pushed Jack Jr gently to the door. The two opened it and left Larry's office.

Larry stood looking at the closed door then sighed and sat down. He idly looked at the check noting the amount. He had really hoped that Jack would be clean. Larry hated telling people bad news, but it was a part of the job. Larry sat back and looked up at the ceiling while wondering what Sara was going to do with that evidence. He sat up he had forgotten to mention the dude who also seemed to be watching Jack and Jay. But he put the thought out of his mind realizing that for one the guy had left following Jay, not Jack when the two left the motel. Secondly, Larry didn't think Sara would answer a call or text from him any time soon. Larry did wonder about the look Sara had given Jack Jr. Maybe he would ride past the house or daycare to make sure the boy didn't all of a sudden develop a case of broken arm or black eyes in the near future. Larry didn't care about the plight of the adults, but children were another story. It wasn't the boy's fault that his father was a cheater and faggot to boot. Larry sat and stared at the ceiling until the phone rang. "Another potential client," he said to the empty office as he reached for the phone.

****

Later that day after sleeping a few hours Calvin was sitting on his couch idly watching the Lakers play the Jazz. He had come to the conclusion that his wonderful plan, formed while nibbling on Samantha's tender bits was foolish at best. How the hell was he going to slip something in Sara's drink? What the hell was he thinking about last night? The answer made Calvin laugh to the empty room over the chatter from the TV. Last night his mind was on the female fountain he had his mouth on. Calvin smirked shaking his head as LeBron James put on a basketball clinic against the Jazz. "I wish I could get some of that gas that they used in *Revolver.*" He thought aloud. Even this thought was mentally brushed off. Calvin realized that the mythical gas would wear off in 10 - 20 minutes at the most. Before he could say Jack Jr, the police would have one of those warnings out. What he needed was time for him to get the boy and unite him with his pops. Once this was done Calvin figured he needed about three to four hours with the two men so he could enjoy the disciplinary action. Then it hit Calvin and he sat up. He was looking at this wrong. He needed to get Jack before he met with the lady or tranny. It would be risky, but if he could snatch Jack up before his rendezvous arrived, he would be able to make it back to Memphis.

Calvin then realized how he could get Jack Jr. Sara usually dropped the boy off around 10:30 or 11:00 and went to the office. "Jack must tell her he is meeting

41

with people or something to have Friday away from the office. Or maybe he goes back around 4:00pm and meets her, then goes home," Calvin mused to himself. Either way that was going to have to be the plan. It would be tight, getting back to the daycare and grabbing the boy. He could snatch him off the playground, but once again the police would be on his ass like a pair of Levi 510 Skinny jeans. Calvin smiled to himself and thought, "Well, if I can't get the boy then at least I will have his daddy for a good five to six hours. That is better than nothing." Calvin laughed and decided the upcoming Friday was the day for payback. He picked up the remote and switched the TV over to DVD. *John Wick* was in the player and Calvin smiled as he imagined him and John taking revenge. "John Wick took his vengeance over a dog. Calvin Hines takes his over money and a slight. Somebody's got to pay, and Jack you are him," Calvin said to himself smiling.

CHAPTER FOUR

"You don't just kill the enemy; you kill his hope by killing his loved ones first. If possible, do this in front of him and watch him wail." - D.P. Black

Calvin decided that Friday was going to be the day. In preparation he had to find a lonely place to take the two Jacks to meter out his punishment. This was an easy task because there was an abandoned house around the block from his. The neighborhood this abandoned house was in consisted of older people who minded their own business. The house was near a space where a developer was putting up some apartment buildings. The noise from the construction site was loud during the day. Calvin figured that since the house was back from the street, and the other houses, it would be perfect for what he planned for Jack and son. Calvin went by the house Monday afternoon to check on the accommodations. Calvin went around to the back of the house and found that the door was padlocked with a flimsy lock. Calvin guessed that the city or whoever didn't care about anyone going into the house. Calvin tested the lock and knew it would be easy to break with a small pair of lock cutters. He looked in the windows and saw that there was some old furniture and a table. "Perfect," he thought as he stood back and looked around the area. The builders down the block were making a lot of racket and the nearest house was two lots away. If Jack howled like a wolf no one would hear him. Calvin left the house. He would come back Thursday night and cut the lock and check how things were inside. There was no need to open the place early, or go in now, and possibly alert a neighbor. Also, he needed to pick up some items from the hardware store. Calvin looked at his watch and decided to go by the day care and watch how Sara picked up Jack Jr. He also wanted a look at the security or cameras that were used at the place. As Calvin headed to his car he decided to first shoot over to West Memphis and check on the camera system at the Motel 8. Calvin didn't see any cameras when he was over there, but that didn't mean that there were none. "Better safe than life in the joint," Calvin thought as he headed to his car.

Some people believe in fate or luck. If there is a such thing then, Jack's fate or luck went bad whereas Calvin should have played the lottery. Calvin's first sign of luck was the information he received from the Motel 8 clerk. Calvin had gone into the lobby and asked how much a room was and what type of security they had. The guy behind the counter was an old white man who was wearing a worn-out Public Enemy shirt. The guy looked like he smoked the wrong substances too much and drank rubbing alcohol. The guy looked at Calvin and told him the price of the room and then let him know that there was a security guard who started at 6pm. Calvin nodded then asked in a conspirator voice, "Do you have cameras videoing the coming and goings of the guests?" The guy laughed and leaned over the desk and said lowly, "The only camera on the premises is the one right up there, videoing our conversation." The man then pointed a dirt bleached finger at the camera in the corner of the lobby. Calvin looked and leaned back away from the smell of the man which reminded him of beer and shit. "None outside?" He asked. "Not a one. If you want a place to meet up and not be seen, this is it," The man said standing back and scratching his behind. Calvin thanked him and went outside. Calvin did a lap around the building in his car scanning for cameras in case the man was wrong but didn't see any. Calvin pulled out of the lot and headed back to Memphis.

As Calvin watched Sara pick up Jack Jr from the day care he shook his head. There was a woman standing outside the place monitoring traffic. Calvin had not seen this woman in the morning. Then he realized that Sara dropped Jack off later than most parents. There was a walkway into the building and the door was behind some tall shrubs. If Sara dropped Jack off and let him walk into the building on his own, Calvin could waylay him behind those shrubs. As Calvin watched the people go in and out of the day care he began to think that Jack Jr may live to see his 18th birthday after all. Calvin didn't see any security cameras outside of the daycare. "With a security guard why would they need one?" He mused as he pulled off and headed to the hardware store. "If I can get him, I will. If not then we'll make do with Senior," Calvin said to the empty car as he headed to Home Depot.

****

Unknown to Calvin, Sara was also in a dilemma. Sara had picked Jack up from jail Sunday and listened to his apology. At first Sara had decided to throw the information Larry had found out into Jack's face and demand a divorce. But, for some reason she didn't. Sara played nice to Jack and said nothing about what she knew. Later that night Jack had wanted to play around but Sara feigned tiredness and that kept Jack at bay. While Jack slept, she looked at his outline in the moonlight. Sara had always liked the way Jack looked while he slept. On this night looking at him sleeping made her retch. She hopped out of bed and went into the bathroom and fought the urge to throw up into the toilet. Sara regained her composure and instead went into the kitchen and opened a bottle of beer. She sat down at the kitchen table and drank the beer thinking.

45

Sara had no intention of getting rid of Jack just when the money was about to come in. She sat and drank thinking that it would be better to wait until Jack signed a movie deal and was making the big money, then leave him. The information Larry had given her would ensure there would be no argument from Jack when she asked for 75 percent of everything. Homosexuality was the in thing in 2020's, but not when you were a public figure and cheating on your wife. Such things were looked down upon in the USA. After all this was a Christian nation. Sara finished her beer and went back to bed. She smiled as she snuggled up under Jack. "Two years max and I'll be living the good life. I may even let him have custody of Jack Jr so I can start over new," she thought as sleep overcame her.

Jack had left home by the time Sara finally rolled out of bed Monday morning. The late-night beer had caused her to sleep late. Jack Jr was up and dressed Sara noted when she went into the kitchen to get some coffee. It was going on 9:30 she observed while pouring herself a cup of coffee. "Jack Jr, are you ready to go to school?" She asked. "Yes Mommy," Jack Jr said not looking up from his iPad. Sara yawned and tasted the coffee. She spit it out in the sink and soon poured the rest down the drain. "Jack and his super strong coffee," Sara said shaking her head. She sat the cup on the counter and went to the refrigerator and opened it. There was a choice between Diet Coke and another beer. Sara found herself leaning towards the beer. The thought of work popped into her head, but she shook it off. She didn't feel like going into the office today. She decided to not go in, but she wasn't going to have Jack Jr following her around all day either. Sara decided to drop him off at daycare and then go have some drinks in Midtown, maybe catch a movie at Studio on The Square. Sara was humming as she went back into the bedroom to shower and get dressed.

Jack got the text from Sara saying she wasn't coming into the office around 11am. His first thought was, "The bitch is seeing another nigga!" Then Jack calmed down. Sara wasn't seeing another man. His foolish outburst this past weekend had almost cost him dearly. Since there were no charges and he wasn't popular enough yet, the incident from Saturday didn't make the papers or internet. Jack had been relieved of this. He knew that it was only a matter of time before PFA Productions offered him a movie deal. He also knew that Semaj Film wanted to offer him a deal. Both of these houses were small, but prosperous. Jack knew the money would be good. The contract offer he was waiting on was from MGM. The other two houses wanted to get him to sign a contract. MGM only wanted the rights to his latest film, *Riodevous*. Jack wanted to sell MGM the rights, for a nice price. That price was going to be seven figures with a small percentage of the royalties. Jack was confident MGM would go for his request. When MGM remade the film using big name stars, the million and small percent of the royalties would be like pennies to the gross taken in at the box office. Sara wouldn't leave him, at least not until the money started coming in. Jack was confident that Sara would forgive his jealous outburst. Sadly, he realized he would have to stop the dallying with Jay but, you have to break a few eggs to make an omelet. Around 2:00pm Jack's phone rang.

At 2:15 Jack ended the call in a daze. Jack looked around the office and was about to holler, "Sara!" When he realized she wasn't there. Jack pumped his fist in the air hollering, "Yes! Yes! Yes!" Jack was aware he sounded like Daniel Bryant the WWE wrestler but didn't care. The call had been from David Green, the head of MGM talent acquisition department. Green had told Jack that MGM wanted the film *Riodevous*. Green went on to tell Jack that they wanted the film ASAP so they could begin casting. Green then asked, "Jack, how much do you need to make this happen. Let's make this quick and to the point. Anything reasonable and it's done." Jack didn't hesitate, "A million and 10 percent of the gross." Green responded, "A million and four and the papers will be in your office tomorrow afternoon." Jack looked at the phone and said,

"Done." "Great. A courier will bring the contracts to your office for your signature. If possible, Jack, have your attorney there to look them over and send the contracts back with the courier." Jack was grinning like an ape. "Will do. Pleasure doing…" Jack never finished because Green had ended the call. That was when Jack went back into his Daniel Bryant impersonation.

Jack again tried Sara's phone to tell her the news, but her phone went straight to voicemail. Jack frowned but shook it off. Jack felt like dancing around the office. Not only was MGM buying the film, but this also meant there was no need for him to finish up his version. This thought saddened him because his version of *Riodevous* was a great piece of directing. Yet he knew it was the script he wrote was what made MGM take notice and want the film. "But that is the way of the film world," he said aloud. Also, with the money MGM offered he could take his film making to a higher level on the next project. It was time to celebrate and since he didn't have to pay for any more postproduction there was a nice piece of money to be spent. Not once did Jack think about calling Calvin and paying him the few thousand dollars that he owed him. Calvin hadn't crossed Jack's mind in weeks.

The person who did come across Jack's mind was Jay. Jack thought of Jay and began getting an erection. Jack looked around the office and called Jay. Jay was between meetings and only had a few minutes to talk. Jay was excited for Jack when he heard the news. "It will be hard for us to meet up from now on," Jay said. Jack knew this, but his erection was talking for him. "I know. But I'm not famous yet. Friday at the M-8?" Jay laughed, "Yeah. One last time. Are you hard Jack?" A moan escaped Jack's mouth as he rubbed the front of his slacks. "Take it out Jack," Jay whispered sexily." Jack moaned, "I already have." Jack was sitting in his desk stroking his now exposed manhood. Jay grinned, "Now you know what to do, and don't let one drop go to waste you naughty boy."

"I won't," Jack said in a voice that sounded more like Jack Jr as he followed instructions like a good boy.

While Jack was first making deals then taking orders from Jay, Sara was at Locale in Midtown. Sara found herself having a nice time in Midtown that afternoon. She had started at Blue Monkey then made her way to Lafayette's where she listened to a few sets by the house band. One old white man in some faded khakis had tried to pick her up. Sara had smiled and told the old guy thanks, but she didn't want to commit murder. By the time Sara walked over to Local to get something to eat she was buzzed. She liked their chicken sandwich and home cut fries. Sara wasn't drunk, but she was mildly high. She pulled out her cell phone and realized that it was almost time to pick up Jack Jr. She also noticed Jack had called a few times. Sara sighed and dialed his number while sitting at the bar debating if she should order to go, or just go pick Jack Jr up and eat later. When Jack answered the phone, he sounded out of breath like he had been running or masturbating. Sara found out she didn't care which one Jack had been doing. When Sara hung up the phone, she was glad she had called. Jack had hit the big time. Sara looked at the phone and decided to wait on eating and pick up Jack Jr. Jack was going to take them out for a big dinner at Flight. Sara didn't want to go smelling like beer and wine. She grabbed her purse and headed for the car. "I may be able to get rid of the fruit in a year," she said smiling as she headed to her car.

****

Late Tuesday morning Calvin was sitting on his back patio checking the lengths of chain he had purchased to see if he had enough to wrap around Jack. Calvin had been by the abandoned house again and saw there were two old folding chairs and what looked like an old moldy living room chair. He didn't go in or stay long just looked through the windows of the house. Calvin was going to use zip ties to keep Jack Jr in place. But he figured when the fun started, Jack senior may bust one of those. The chains and padlock were another story. Unless Jack was some Memphis version of the Hulk, the chains would keep him secured just fine. Calvin nodded as he finished checking the chain and the padlocks. He wished he had a strait jacket but, they cost big money and could be traced. The chain and padlocks would do just fine. Calvin looked at the list he had written and checked to be sure he had all of the tools he was going to need to ensure the two Jacks had a merry time before meeting Satan. Well, the elder Jack would meet him. Calvin supposed Jack Jr was still a child and was pure so he may meet the white Jesus.

Calvin looked at the supplies and mentally checked them off of his list: wire cutters, two box cutters, box of replacement blades, zip ties, hack saw, package of hacksaw blades, hammer, box of three-inch nails, propane torch, propane refill. Calvin double checked the list and nodded. He then put the items in a black duffle bag he used when going on shoots to carry equipment. "No need to worry about a job, right Jack?" Calvin said and he picked up the wire cutters and looked at them while imagining what he was going to use them for. Calvin put the wire cutters in the bag and stood up stretching his back. There were a few more items he needed to pick up for the Friday Day Party he was planning. He wanted to get these items today so he could do a few dry runs of the plan Wednesday. "Everything has to be timed and precise Jackie boy," Calvin laughed as he went into the house.

****

While Calvin was preparing party favors, Jack and Sara were in heaven. For the first time in years Jack and Sara had ridden to work together. Jack Jr was also at the office with his parents. Jack wanted to share his signing the MGM deal with his family. Sara had on a smart tan pants suit with heels. Jack was wearing a deep brown Calvin Klein suit and some Aldo ankle boots. Jack traded his tie for a creme ascot. Jack Jr. had on some black slacks and a white and green Polo shirt along with some black Stride Rite loafers. The whole family was upbeat. It wasn't log after they arrived at the office when the courier came in followed by Jack's lawyer, David Carter. Sara had asked the courier if he wanted something to drink. The guy said no and took a seat in one of the chairs across from Sara's desk. Jack had taken the package from the courier and headed into the small area of the office where his desk was along with a small table with four chairs. Jack Jr was sitting at the table playing on his iPad. Jack, David and Sara took seats. Jack was looking at the packet in his hand. Sara said, "Open it Jack and let us see. David needs to check the contract before you sign it. I doubt that courier wants to sit in the front office all day." Jack looked at her as if coming out of a dream and opened the packet. Jack scanned the papers then handed them to David. Jack was grinning.

David scanned the contract with knowing eyes. He had done work for MGM before and knew how they worded certain phrases. David sat looking at the contract for a good 20 minutes in silence. Jack and Sara sat quietly waiting on David's verdict. Even Jack Jr seemed to be waiting because he was looking at the adults instead of his iPad. David nodded and grunted sitting back while arranging the papers on the table. "Well?" Jack asked. David looked at Sara and Jack Jr then back at Jack. "Jack, you are on your way. The deal is just like you said you wanted and what Green agreed to. Get your pen and sign here." David pointed to a line on the last page. "Warm up your copy machine so we'll have a copy and send this back to MGM. The money will be paid upon receipt of the contract being finalized in five business days." Jack looked at Sara and was speechless. In five days, he would have a million dollars. While Jack seemed to be in a state of shock, Sara wasn't. Sara had already stood up and went to the copy machine and turned it on so it would be ready. "Hurry up Jack and sign the paper. No need to let the grass grow under your feet!" This statement brought laughter to both David and Jack, as Jack signed the contract.

A few minutes later the courier was gone, and Jack, Sara and David were standing in the front office. David congratulated Jack and told him he had to get back to the office. "Jack with this deal other movie houses will be knocking on your door," David told Jack and Sara as he opened the door. "I know. Let them come as long as they bring their check book!" Jack said laughing while looking at Sara who was smiling too. David laughed and left. Jack and Sara stood first looking at the door and then each other. "We made it Sara!" Jack said grabbing her up in a fierce hug. Sara stiffened then relaxed into the hug, "Yes you have Jack." She leaned back and looked up into his face smiling. "Now we can move into the neighborhood we have wanted to all along," she said. "We will build us our own neighborhood before I'm done Sara," he replied then kissed her deeply. Jack Jr stood there watching for a few seconds then said, "Will we still be able to eat Churches on Wednesday?" Sara looked at Jack and they both started to laugh bringing a confused look to Jack Jr's face. "I like Churches chicken," Jack Jr said looking at the two laughing adults.

The next day, Wednesday, MGM dropped a small press tidbit stating the rights to the film *Riodevous* had been acquired from Jack Davis for an undisclosed sum. Paul, who always read all the big movie houses X feeds and website posts, saw the news on MGM's X account. Paul wondered if Jack had ever paid Calvin. If he hadn't, he sure could afford to now with the money from MGM. Paul called Calvin to ask him if he ever got paid. Calvin was going through his second dry run and was glad he was doing these practice runs. He found that the timing really depended on the flow and density of traffic. Calvin had no doubt he would be able to grab Jack. The window of opportunity to grab Jack Jr was what was worrying Calvin. He was driving back to Jack's house for another dry run when he took Paul's call.

"Calvin what's up?" Paul asked. "Nothing much Paul. How are you doing?" Calvin replied while watching traffic in front of him. "Great. Did you ever get paid by Jack?" Paul asked. "No. I chalked that up to the game," Calvin replied attempting to sound upbeat and nonchalant. "Well, maybe he will now that he had sold the rights to that film to MGM," Paul replied cooly. "What?" Calvin asked loudly. "Yep, dude sold the rights sometime this week for an undisclosed amount," Paul replied. Calvin fought hard to keep bitterness out of his reply. He didn't want anyone to have any concept of bitterness he felt towards Jack. "Man, that's good for him! I am going to have to call or text him congratulations!" Paul looked at the phone in shock and a little disgust. Paul had wanted Calvin to get mad and go off about not being paid by Jack. That type of reaction would have been something to gossip about with his wife and her friends. Instead, here was Calvin congratulating a man who fucked him out of a couple grand and that reference. Paul replied dryly, "Yeah, I thought you would be excited about this." "I am Paul! Let me text him now. Thanks for letting me know. Later." Calvin ended the call.

Calvin was past hot anger at Jack. Calvin's anger had cooled to the point of freezing. As he turned onto Jack's block for another dry run, he had a thin smile on his face.

Thursday neither Jack nor Sara made it to the office. Wednesday evening Jack had treated his family to another extravagant meal, this time at Folks Folly. The meal had included several glasses of wine for him and Sara. By the time the family had made it home, Jack Jr was asleep in the backseat. Jack was slightly drunk, and Sara was drunk. Jack carried Jack Jr into the house while Sara had gone in and cut on the entertainment system and began blasting *Anaconda*. Jack went into Juniors room pulled Jack Jr's shoes off and put him in the bed.

When Jack went into the kitchen, Sara was drinking a beer and singing off key to the lyrics. Jack grinned and opened the refrigerator and grabbed him a beer and opened it. He took a deep swig while watching Sara

who was now dancing in place drunkenly. Jack had a
sudden flash of horniness as he watched Sara's plump
behind sway. Jack watched Sara for another minute and
when the song changed to *Lemonade,* he downed the rest
of his beer. He tore his pants open as he lurched towards
Sara. His mind was only on her swaying hips and the
fleshy cheeks of her behind. Sara felt him coming up
behind her and relaxed. She had decided to fuck him that
night because she was horny, drinking made her that way.
When Sara felt his breath on her neck and his hands
fumbling for her waist and zipper, she held her arms up.
Jack sensing capitulation tore her pants off and ripped her
panties. Sara said, "Lube me up first, and not with
Vaseline." Jack dropped to the floor and parted Sara's
cheeks and got to work.

Thursday morning found Jack laying in the kitchen
with his pants around his ankles on his back snoring. The
floor around Jack's head was damp and his face was also.
Sara, on the other hand, was in the bedroom sleeping
soundly in her bed. The previous night, Sara left Jack in
the kitchen and went to bed properly. When they had
finished the wild encounter in the kitchen the previous
night Sara had stood looking down on Jack with a face full
of drunken contempt. "Faggot," she said as she swayed
looking down on him. Jack had rolled over onto his back
and started snoring with his mouth wide open. Sara had
felt the need to urinate and was about to head into the
bathroom. Instead, she shrugged and proceeded to squat
over Jack's open mouth. "Waste not want not," Sara said
drunkenly.

The next morning Jack was snoring loudly when
Jack Jr came into the kitchen to get some water. Jack Jr
ran into his parent's bedroom hollering that his father was
dead, waking Sara. Sara popped up, "Jack Jr stop that
yelling!" "Daddy is dead in the kitchen!" He shouted.
Sara listened and could hear Jack snoring. "He's not dead.
He just had too much fun last night. Go back to your room
and lay down or play on your iPad. Mommy will come get

you in a while." Jack Jr nodded and went back into his room. Sara lay back down and promptly fell asleep. It was 11:30 when she woke up.

Jack had woken up at 9:30. His head was hurting, and he had a salty taste in his mouth. He sat up in the kitchen and looked around. "Man, that wine has some kick to it," He mumbled while holding his head. He rose from the floor shakily and realized his pants were still around his ankles. He pulled his pants up wincing at the stab of pain that went through his forebrain. Jack went and sat on the couch in the living room to get his bearings and to stop the spinning feeling in his skull. He lay back and closed his eyes. Jack was awakened three hours later by Sara who was looking tired and shaking his arm. "You want something from Chik-fil-A?" She asked him. Jack Jr was standing by her looking at him curiously. "Some nuggets and a sandwich," Sara nodded and turned away followed by Jack Jr. Jack decided the couch was extremely comfortable and stretched out on his side with his feet hanging off one end and went to sleep. It was dark when he finally got up and showered.

Calvin was on a mission Thursday. While Jack and Sara recuperated from the previous night's overindulgence, Calvin was working. Calvin decided to go and open up the house during the day. This way he could see if anyone would notice him or bother him. Calvin felt it would be better to be accused of burglary than caught red handed committing murder. Calvin's luck was on again. He opened the back door and was in the house with no one the wiser. Once inside Calvin saw that the table and chairs were dusty, but sturdy enough to serve his purpose. There was no electricity, but what he was planning would be finished before the sun set. He wouldn't need any light to drag the bodies out and put them into his car once the sun went down. For that task Calvin wanted it to be dark. Once he finished getting the house prepared Calvin went to the woods off 240. This was the part of the task that would be tricky. Calvin would have to take his time while heading off into the wooded area. He knew where he wanted to put the bodies. Getting the truck there without drawing attention was going to be a challenge.

Calvin pulled over on the shoulder paused, then simply turned into the woods. He was driving his old Ram truck. What Calvin didn't want was the police to drive by and wonder what he was doing. Calvin knew this area and the trails because he had been four wheeling with his friend Harry. Harry had two four wheelers and let Calvin ride one when they went out. Calvin made the turn into the woods without any problem. It was then that Calvin realized that no one really cared about people on the side of the road. Especially ones who were driving into the woods. Anyone who noticed him would think he was another off-road enthusiast doing some off roading. Calvin drove about a mile in and parked. He got out and walked the rest of the way. The spot he chose was secluded and the trees were close together. There wasn't much chance of anyone finding the bodies or catching him burying them either. Calvin looked around and nodded. He had thought about digging the grave today but decided against it. An open grave may rouse suspicion if it was found. He was pretty sure no one would find the grave, but why risk it? By the time Calvin got to this point in his plan, he would be on the downside, as they say, and could take his time and bury the dead the right way. Deep and covered. Calvin was humming as he headed back to the truck. As he pulled off, he realized he felt anxious. Calvin felt like a child waiting for Christmas to open presents. Calvin found he both liked and hated that feeling.

CHAPTER FIVE

"Once the killing starts there is nothing left to do but keep going until everyone is dead." - David Kincaid

Friday morning started normal for Jack. He got out of bed at 7:30 am and went and took a long piss. Jack was notorious for taking long showers and using up the hot water, so he always got up an hour before Sara. Jack took his usual 20-minute shower after shaving and brushing his teeth. After his shower he made himself a cup of coffee and sat at the kitchen table thinking about nothing for another 10 minutes. When he rose, he finished his coffee and rinsed out the cup placing it in the dish holder. Jack went back into the bedroom thinking about what he would do when he got the million next week. As he ran through a list of things while dressing it hit him. "I can pay Calvin. Maybe give him a bonus since I screwed him on that reference situation," he thought as he buttoned up his shirt. Technically as far as Sara was concerned, he had already paid Calvin.

Jack smiled to himself as he headed into the small office he used to work from home. The memory of what Calvin's money had really been spent on brought an erection into his pants. Jack sat down and took the checkbook he used for business and wrote out a check to

Calvin for 3,500 dollars. Jack pulled out his wallet then paused, "No. I will put it in an envelope to make it look more professional." With the envelope in his hand Jack went and took his jacket out of the closet and put the envelope in the inside pocket. "I'll stop by his place and give this to him after I finish up with Jay. I'll be tying up all loose ends in preparation for a new life," Jack said as he left out of the house. In the bedroom Sara let out a loud wet fart as Jack closed the door.

While Jack was leaving his house at 9:30 am, Calvin was already sitting in the Burger King lot next to the Motel 8. Calvin was drinking an orange juice from Burger King thinking, "This shit is nothing but colored water." Calvin had been up since five AM going through the plan and checking his equipment. Calvin had ridden by the abandoned house but didn't get out. He cruised through the alley behind the house and saw nothing out of place, so he kept going. Calvin took another sip of the orange water, as he had come to think of the drink, and looked at the clock. He was in his car. He decided to snatch Jack and Jack Jr in his car instead of the truck. For one, his car, a Chevy Impala, had a nice size trunk. If Jack or his son woke up, they would still be in the trunk. If worse came to worse, he would simply shoot his trunk up. That method of murder would not be as satisfying, but it would suffice. Calvin had no intention of wrestling with Jack while his son screamed and bit his leg.

Calvin glanced at the blackjack he had sitting in the passenger seat. That was how he was going to cool Jack off. He would probably do the same for Jack Jr too. It would be easier to take two unconscious people into the abandoned house instead of two awakened ones. The clock on the dash read 9:15 am. Calvin took another sip of the orange water and started the car. He drove into the Motel 8 lot and parked a few car lengths over from where he had seen Jack park before. Calvin sat and waited. His first plan was to grab Jack on his way out of the office after getting the room. Calvin changed from that plan. Instead, he planned on waylaying Jack on the way into the office. Calvin's plan was good to him and would get Jack positioned to be taken. Calvin glanced at the clock, then looked at the orange water and decided against another drink. Right when he was about to pick up the orange water and take a sip, he saw Jack's car about to turn into the lot. Calvin popped the trunk and got out of his car and went to the trunk and raised it. Calvin never took his eyes off of Jack's car as Jack turned into the lot and pulled up in a spot three spaces from Calvin. Calvin grinned as he watched Jack turn off the car. Calvin patted his back pocket to be sure he had the blackjack. When Jack got out Calvin hollered to him.

"Jack! Jack! Man! What a life saver!" Calvin hollered to the surprised Jack who was closing his car door. Jack looked at the man calling his name confused, then realized it was Calvin and relaxed. Jack looked around and started walking to where Calvin was standing by his car with the trunk up. "Calvin? Calvin what are you doing at a motel this early in the morning?" Jack asked as he walked over by Calvin. "I would guess it is the same thing you are doing at one Jack," Calvin said grinning slyly. Jack nodded and shrugged. Calvin went on, "Man I need some help with this," Calvin pointed into the trunk. Jack was looking around being careful that no one noticed him, or that Jay wasn't pulling into the lot. Jack did not want Calvin to know that he was messing around with a man. These thoughts were distracting Jack's attention and made him unfocused to the fact that Calvin was pointing at nothing in his trunk. Jack turned and looked into the trunk still thinking about being seen or Jay pulling up. Jack bent over the trunk to see better when Calvin brought the blackjack down on the back of his head. "There it is Jack! Can you see it!" Jack couldn't see anything much less respond. Calvin had knocked him unconscious with one blow. Calvin looked around and grabbed Jack and put him all the way into the trunk. Calvin shoved a gag in his open mouth and used two zip ties to tie his hands behind his

back and his feet together. Calvin was sweating from
effort and speed. Calvin looked at the unconscious Jack
and began to shut the trunk, then stopped. Calvin picked up
the blackjack out of the trunk and cracked Jack one more
time on his head to be sure he was out. Calvin, then
searched Jack's pockets and grabbed his keys while
overlooking the envelop in his coat pocket. Things may
have turned out different if Calvin had of opened that
envelop.

Calvin was ad libbing at this point and he knew
time was tight. He slipped on some thin plastic gloves as
he walked. Calvin quickly got in Jack's car. He started it
up and drove it around the back of the Motel 8 and parked
it by a dumpster. This way when Jack's lover came into
the lot, he would think Jack hadn't gotten there yet. After
some time, Jack's lover would think he had been stood up.
Calvin hustled back to the front of the lot and was getting
into his car when he saw the car the man had driven turn
into the lot. Calvin hurriedly started his car and pulled off
as the man parked in the spot Jack's car had just been in.
Calvin looked the other way as he pulled off, so the man
wouldn't see his face. As Calvin pulled into traffic he
glanced at the car. The man was putting on lipstick or
something while looking into a compact. Calvin laughed,
"He will have to dildo his own ass today. Jack has other
plans." Calvin turned on the radio as he merged onto 40
East. He glanced at the clock. It read 9:55 am. Calvin
pushed down on the gas. It would be tight at best to get
Jack Jr. The gambit with the car cost him time. But at least
he had Senior to take out his anger on. Calvin smiled
happily as he crossed the bridge heading into Memphis.

Calvin's luck was lottery winner proportions that
Friday. Sara had gotten up in a bad mood. Sara had been
awake since 8:00 am but decided to stay in bed until Jack
left. Part of Sara's moodiness came from a bad dream she
had during the night. Sara had dreamed that she was older,
or at least she thought she was. She had been sitting in the
plush living room of an extremely nice house. Sara

understood or felt that this was her home and was relaxing when the doorbell rang. When she opened the door there were two teenagers standing in the entrance kissing passionately. Sara had said, "Excuse me, but this is not the Hilton. Go get a room and stop bothering people." She was closing the door when the teenage girl, dressed in a high school cheerleading outfit said, "Mommy it is me, Jack Jr!" Sara stopped closing the door and gaped at the girl. The girl seemed to be about 17 or 18 years old. Sara noticed the girl had some nice breasts and was making the cheerleader outfit look sexy, not teen cheery at all. The outfit on this person who said they were her son looked the way a porn star would wear a cheerleader outfit before an intense anal sex scene. Sara scanned the girl's body again this time noticing the way the skirt seemed to be barely covering the edge of her panties. Sara also noted the deep cut of the top which resembled no cheer leading outfit she had ever seen before. Sara looked at the teenage boy. The boy was typical white trash. He had on some big boots that seemed to be a mix between engineer boots and cowboy boots. Sara couldn't tell because they seemed to be covered in mud or possibly shit. The jeans the boy was wearing were also spotted with either mud or shit. Sara had seen homeless people who looked cleaner. The jeans were topped by a t-shirt that had a faded Colt 45 Malt Liquor label on it. The young man's face was surrounded by a beard that looked at home on *Duck Dynasty*. The young man, or hillbilly as Sara was beginning to think of him, was grinning and exposing two gold teeth and some yellow ones. The hillbilly's eyes were blue and too close together for Sara's liking. The one thing that seemed out of place, because it looked clean, was the hillbilly's hair. The hillbilly had shocking blonde almost white hair. "How do Ma'am. I really like your daughter," The hillbilly said extending his hand. Sara looked at the hand in disgust noticing the filth under the nails. Before Sara could say anything, the person claiming to be Jack Jr spoke up, "Isn't he great Mommy!" This shook Sara out of the mind fugue

61

which seemed to be coming over her thought process, "I don't know who the hell you are, but you are not coming in here! Jack! Jack, come down here right now!" Sara stood barring the door to the consternation of Jack Jr and the embarrassment of the hillbilly. Sara felt someone come up behind her. The person claiming to be Jack Jr brightened at the sight of the newcomer, "Daddy!" Sara glowered, "Shut that shit up! My son Jack Jr is out hanging with his friends and probably screwing some females right now! Furthermore…" "Furthermore, Jack Jr is right here on our doorstep and I'm wondering why he and this handsome young man haven't been let in?" The voice sounded like Jack but higher, more effeminate. Sara turned and started screaming as she looked into the face of Jack with makeup, eyeliner, and loud red lip plumper lipstick on. Jack had a red, white and blue long weave done up like Peg on that old TV show, *Married with Children*. Sara's screams increased when she looked down and saw the enlarged breasts poking like they were going to burst out of the Memphis Grizzly tube shirt dress Jack was wearing. Before she could see more, she had shouted herself awake from the dream. Sara woke up with a scream behind her lips as she lay in the bed beginning to realize that it was all a dream.

Sara lay in the bed looking up at the ceiling before hot tears of frustration rolled down her cheeks. "Why? Why did this have to happen to her?" She thought bitterly as she heard Jack leave out of the house. Sara stared into the morning light hating Jack and beginning to wonder about Jack Jr. Sara rose when she heard the boy getting up and going into the bathroom. "I'll bet he's sitting down to piss," she thought viciously and let out a harsh mean laugh. Sara was not in a good mood when she and Jack Jr left heading to the daycare two hours later.

Calvin was hustling to get to the daycare but resigned to the fact he probably would not make it. The clock on the dashboard read 10:20 and he still had to park and get into position to grab Jack Jr. Calvin had decided to simply park in the back of the daycare in one of the spots close to the building. Calvin hadn't decided on how he was going to grab Jack Jr. If Jack Jr started to scream, he was going to get the blackjack right then and there. If he came along willingly, then Jack Jr's head would meet the blackjack by the car. Calvin decided to run back to the car and speed off if someone came out and asked what he was doing out there before he grabbed Jack Jr. Calvin had removed his license plate on the back and replaced it with a fake license applied for paper he had printed off the internet. Any person who may see him leaving may note the car but, there were plenty of Impala's around Memphis. Since he would not have officially committed a crime, Calvin wasn't worried about MPD seriously looking for him. Calvin pulled into the back lot and looked at the clock. It read, 10:27 am. Calvin got out of the car and casually walked to the front of the building.

While Calvin was walking to the front of the building Sara was turning onto the block of the daycare. Sara's mood had worsened on the drive to the daycare. Sara was thinking about Jack and his lover. She had called the office with no answer. Sara was about to call his cell phone, when she remembered the motel Larry had told her Jack met the man at. Sara was sure as shit that Jack was probably meeting the man again at the same hotel. Why would he change up? Sara was anxious and tense when she pulled up at the daycare. She started to get out but changed her mind. "Jack Jr, be a big boy and walk to the center on your own. You know how to open the door. Tell Ms. Chase I had to run. See you later baby." Jack Jr was elated his mother wasn't mad at him and said, "Okay Mommy. I'll see you later." Jack Jr felt like a big boy as he closed the door and headed towards the daycare. Sara glanced at Jack Jr's retreating figure and thought, "The boy isn't bad. I'll keep him with me and stick Jack for support." Sara watched Jack Jr take five or six steps, then pulled off not looking back. If Sara had of glanced into her review mirror, she would at least have had one last look at Jack Jr alive or dead.

Calvin was just making it to the front of the daycare when he saw Sara's car pull off. "Damn! I missed him," Calvin said bitterly and began to turn around when Jack Jr stepped into view. Jack Jr came around the hedges into Calvin's sight and was about to stop and lord only knows what when Calvin, elated and excited, pounced on him and clubbed him unconscious. Calvin grabbed up the boy then carrying him like a football raced to the back of the daycare. "That wasn't the plan," he thought running towards the car. Calvin triggered the trunk and briefly thought, "What if Jack's awake?" He brushed the thought away laughing because if he was, he couldn't move with his hands and feet bound. Calvin got to the trunk and raised it up and tossed Jack Jr on top of his still unconscious dad. Calvin slammed the trunk and looked around. His heart was racing, but it calmed when he saw no one was outside and no one was looking out of a window. Calvin calmly walked to the driver side and got in. Calvin drove off slowly. As he drove past the daycare, he casually looked at the building. No one had come out to raise an alarm because it was past the time children were expected, except when parents brought them in. Calvin cut on the radio and headed to the abandoned house while Bruno Mars sang about chunky females.

****

When Jack regained consciousness, he knew he was in trouble before he opened his eyes. Jack could feel the chains around his chest and legs. He was laying naked in nothing but his underwear. Jack thought, "Please let this be a dream." The sound of Jack Jr screaming made his eyes jump open and destroyed any thoughts of his situation being a dream. When Jack opened his eyes, he looked up into Calvin's grinning face. "What the fuck am I doing here Calvin!" He asked the grinning upside-down face. The face kept grinning and rose up and Jack felt the wind being driven out of his lungs from a boot to the stomach.

Jack writhed on the floor gasping for breath and dry retching. Calvin smiled down evilly as he watched Jack writher in pain on the dirty faded linoleum floor. The builders down the block were making such a racket that Calvin was in no fear of anyone hearing Jack's screams. Calvin planned on giving Jack a lot to scream about.

Calvin turned away while Jack tried to throw up his morning coffee and went into the other room. Jack Jr was lying on the floor whimpering around a dirty rag Calvin had found in the house. How Jack Jr had managed to scream or even make loud noises was beyond Calvin. Calvin was humming tunelessly as he approached the boy whose eyes looked the size of softballs. Calvin smiled and bent down and removed the rag. Jack Jr began to spit as if trying to get something unpleasant out of his mouth. Calvin looked at the rag and shrugged because it looked like there was some form of grease, or maybe even shit on the rag. Thinking of the latter he tossed the rag aside. "Do you love your Daddy boy?" Calvin asked in a soothing voice. Jack Jr had stopped spitting and was beginning to cry. "Yes!" Jack Jr wailed. "I do love him. Daddy! Daddy!" Jack Jr cried out. Calvin smiled as he watched the boy wail thinking, "Damn this boy got a water head." Calvin grinned broader when he heard, "Jack? Jack Jr, are you here?" Jack was calling to the boy in a pained, gasping voice. "Yes, Daddy I'm here. I'm scared! Come get me!" Jack Jr cried out seeming to forget the grinning man leaning over him. Sadly, for both Jacks the grinning man didn't forget about them.

As Jack Jr cried for Jack, Calvin pulled his leather belt off and wrapped it around his fist. As Jack Jr wailed Calvin stood and brought the foot of heavy leather crashing down across Jack Jr's eyes. The sound of the smack echoed through the house like the sound of a bullwhip hitting a side of pork. Jack paused then howled, "Jack Jr! Jr!" Jack Jr couldn't hear his father because he was howling. Calvin's lips were peeled back from his teeth and the sound of Jack Jr howling almost drove him into a frenzy. Calvin lashed Jack Jr twice more then, caught himself. Jack Jr was screaming to the point where there were no sounds coming out of his mouth. Calvin could hear Jack in the next room sobbing and cursing, "You mother fucker! You mother fucker! Leave my son alone!" The final sentence came out a sobbing plea. Calvin closed his eyes and gathered himself as he looked down on the crying Jack Jr whose face was swelling up like a bumpy inner tube. Calvin went and grabbed the dirty rag and shoved it in Jack Jr's mouth stifling the moans that were coming from the boy's mouth. Calvin stood and drew his leg back to kick the boy, then thought better of it and turned and went into the other room.

Jack was looking at Calvin with tears streaming down his cheeks. "Why? Why Calvin?" Jack sobbed. Calvin frowned and went over and kicked Jack so hard in the gut that Jack slid across the room gasping. "Now, now Jackie Baby. We'll get to that soon enough," Calvin turned away and reached into the duffel bag he had brought in. Calvin pulled two feet of razor wire out of the bag that had a thick piece of leather taped around one end. Calvin grabbed the leather end and swung it back and forth. Jack had stopped gasping when he heard the swishing sound the razor wire made. As Calvin started walking towards Jack he was grinning again.

Jack saw the razor wire and started trying to break the chains, to no avail. "Calvin stop! Stop! In God's name man stop!" Jack shouted. Calvin paused as if thinking. "No. No, I don't think I will stop. I am going forth in my name." Jack started squirming like a guy doing that old break dance move, "The Worm." Calvin smiled as he brought the razor wire slashing down on Jack's bucking back. Jack stopped squirming as the razor wire met his flesh. All thoughts of getting away were replaced by thoughts of pain. Intense pain.

****

Calvin sat in the old rickety chair relaxing as he looked at Jack's mangled back. Calvin has lashed Jack's back like a lunatic dominatrix getting off on a client. Calvin had started off targeting the back but had moved down and lashed Jack's buttocks so his whole lower torso was red. Jack's underwear was a shredded ruin of red gore drenched cloth. Jack's back was a raw wound. He sat listening for noise from the room Jack Jr was in. There was none. Calvin supposed the boy had heard his father yelling and was now too paranoid with fear to do anything. "Jack you just enjoy your nap. I have to go tighten up Junior," Calvin said to Jack's unconscious form. Calvin sighed, "Jack, you need Ritalin to keep you focused." He was laughing as he went into the next room.

Sure enough, Jack Jr was laying silent. Calvin burst out laughing as he looked at Jack Jr's eyes. They reminded him of a crack head who was geeking. Calvin marveled at how the boy's eyes could be so big with all the welp marks on his face from the belt. Calvin tossed the razor wire onto the floor in front of the boys bulging eyes and went back into the room where he noted that Jack was still getting his beauty sleep. Calvin reached into the duffel bag and rambled around until he pulled out a small hammer. Calvin looked at the items in the bag and sighed, "I won't get to use some of the good stuff like the shock therapy but…" He reached into the bag and pulled out a bottle of rubbing alcohol. Jack was beginning to stir and moan. Calvin went over to Jack and shook him with his foot. Jack winced and screamed as he tried to move opening up the gory wound that was his back. "I hear you Jack," Calvin said nodding down into Jack's pain riven face. Jack was laying on his side and being careful to not roll onto his back. Calvin snatched Jack by the shoulder and forced him onto his stomach with his left hand. Jack began kicking, but all movement stopped when Calvin poured the bottle of rubbing alcohol onto Jack's back. Calvin stood up gasping, "Jack we can't have infection setting in. You supposed to clean cuts and abrasions."

Calvin realized Jack had blacked out again and shook his head. "Some people have no tolerance for pain," he said turning away and grabbing the hammer before heading into the other room.

Calvin leaned over by Jack Jr's sweating face. "Let's play a game Jack Jr." Jack Jr was shaking head and beginning to cry. Calvin smiled as he pulled the boys shoes and socks off exposing his feet. Calvin looked at Jack Jr's crying face. "You ever play, This Little Piggy?" Jack Jr was shaking his head no. Calvin smiled soothingly as he rubbed Jack Jr's feet and toes. He briefly thought of going and getting the wire cutters, but reserved those for Jack Sr. Calvin pushed Jack Jr against the wall and used his left hand to hold the boys left foot against the wall. He rubbed the hammer over the boy's toes bringing shrieks from him. "This little piggy was bad!" Calvin grunted as he swung the hammer with all his might. By the time Calvin got to the third piggy, Jack Jr was sleeping and dreaming with his father.

****

Calvin was humming as he left out of the abandoned building. The day had gone well. Jack had performed well, and Jack Jr had played his role brilliantly. Calvin looked around as he exited the yard and cut across the alley heading to his house to get the truck. Calvin looked at his phone. It was almost 3pm. He figured that the only person who would be looking for Jack and Jack Jr would be Sara. Jack's car would not cause a stir at the hotel until maybe Sunday. Jack Jr missing though would cause quite a stir. Even that would be forestalled as the authorities would want to contact Jack before launching a full-scale search for the boy. Even if the police did start a search right away, where would they begin? Calvin had snatched the boy without being seen and no signs of a struggle. The police would probably start searching the neighborhood that the daycare was in. The abandoned house was not even in the same part of town. Calvin was sure that he would be able to get the evidence in a nice patch of unmarked ground long before the police even began to form a hypothesis about what happened to Jack Jr.

As Calvin turned into his yard he had to grin. In the movies people woke up and escaped while their abductor went to get a cup of coffee or eat. Calvin made sure that wouldn't happen. He had made sure Jack's chains were still secure and even zip tied Jack Jr with new ties before he left. Calvin had also shoved gags in both Jack's mouths and secured them by wrapping duct tape around their heads. He was taking no chances. Calvin was quite sure Jack Jr would only be taking in the Hereafter. Jack Sr, well Calvin had taken measures to ensure that if he was found in the house he wouldn't be talking, or doing much of anything, for months. Yet, even with his precautions Calvin found himself, not rushing, but moving at a rapid pace as he went to the truck and checked the truck bed. There was an old comforter he had found in a garbage dumpster awhile back. This would be used to cover the two Jacks as he escorted them to their final resting place. Calvin fired up the truck and pulled out of the driveway heading back to the abandoned house. He wanted to be finished with this sordid mess by 9 pm in time to stop by Local and have a few beers.

****

When Jack regained consciousness, he found himself looking up from what seemed to be a chasm. Calvin appeared at the head of the chasm and was looking down at him. Before Jack could say anything, pain shot through him from everywhere. Jack's legs felt like the bones were broken and if he tried to move, he felt bones grinding together. He tried to reach down to check his chest and realized it was the same with his arms. Jack inhaled to ask Calvin something and pain shot through his chest. Jack realized that his ribs and sternum were likely broken and badly. Yet, he could not faint or black out. Calvin seemed to read Jack's thought. "Jack, I needed you alert for this part of our party. I gave you a potent dose of stimulants in the form of uppers and cocaine to ensure your alertness." Jack knew there was some truth to what Calvin was saying because his heart was racing. "Why," Jack croaked up at the grinning Calvin. "Remember that reference request I asked you about Jack? Well, you didn't do it and it cost me a job that I needed. On top of that Jack, you never paid me my money. Not only did you betray a trust, but you also welched as they say," Calvin said quietly with anger boiling in his tone. Jack's pain addled mind understood and he croaked, "Calvin, the money...". Calvin cut him off. "Jack the money was a small item. That reference would have gotten me a documentary job that would have paid well and put my companies name on a national level. You fucked me. So, I fucked you back." Calvin stood and saluted Jack with a flourish. "To show I am not an unfair man I am not going to kill you. I will give you a fair chance to escape. I am going to bury you breathing. If you can get out, I will take you to the hospital. You have to move fast though, Jackie Baby. Your air will run out in 2-3 minutes." Calvin started to shovel dirt down on Jack then, stopped as Jack groaned. "Calvin!" Calvin looked into the grave. "Oh, I will even supply you with some company on your way to freedom or to heaven." Calvin stepped away and came back with Jack Jr. Jack groaned as he saw the boy looking down into the grave. It was the odd shape of Jack Jr's head that made Jack realize that Jack Jr was dead. Jack Jr's head was literally collapsed on one side. The reason Jack Jr's eyes were open was because he had no eyelids. They had been cut off. Calvin tossed the cadaver down and the body fell on top of Jack. The brutalized head was even with Jack own face and the open staring eyes were boring into his own. Jack began to scream and trying to move to no avail. His arms and legs were broken, and Jack Jr's body was lying on top of him, pushing his crushed sternum and ribs down into his organs. Jack looked at the staring eyes of Jack Jr and began to scream.

Calvin laughed and said, "It's either goodbye Jack or see you soon." Calvin began to shovel dirt onto the two Jacks while singing, "Leaning on the everlasting arms..."

EPILOGUE

"There is nothing so satisfying as a job well done." - A Fool

Calvin went back to the abandoned house and poured gasoline over the floors in the rooms where Jack and Jack Jr had been. Calvin saturated the two Jack's clothes to ensure they would burn. He looked into the rooms to be sure that the bloody areas were well soaked in gas and then lit a pack of matches on fire. Calvin threw the matches onto the kitchen floor and rushed out the door. Calvin ran down the block away from his house. He didn't think anyone would see him. If anyone did see him, they would view the arsonist as he ran the other way, not towards Calvin's block. Calvin ran and turned two blocks away and got into his truck where he had parked it. Calvin fired up the truck and drove off. He drove by the abandoned house and was pleased to see flames coming from the windows. A crowd was gathering. No one seemed to be too concerned since the house was a derelict. Calvin turned and headed towards Local. It was 9:30pm and he could grab some beers and maybe a chicken sandwich. All thoughts of Jack and Jack Jr were leaving his head like the way the flames consumed the evidence in that abandoned house. Ironically, inside of Jack's coat that was now

72

burning merrily, was the check Jack had made out to Calvin for his services.

****

Earlier that day Sara had gone to the Motel 8 and drove through the lot looking for Jack's car. Sara was so intent on the cars that were parked by the building that when she drove around the back, she missed Jack's car parked by the dumpster. Sara went back into the front and parked. Sara waited to see if Jack would show for about an hour before leaving. Sara wondered if Jack had met up with his lover at another hotel as she crossed the bridge into Tennessee.

Sara wasn't the only one who waited for Jack at the Motel 8. Jay had gotten there and rented a room. Jay had sat in the room for three hours waiting on Jack. Finally disgusted that Jack didn't answer his texts or phone he had checked out and left. Jay was upset with Jack and decided to let him know about it when he finally got in touch with him.

Calvin was correct. Jack's car wasn't discovered until that Sunday. It was discovered by the clerk who had unknowingly given Calvin the information needed to pull off the crime. The clerk went to dump the garbage from the office and smoke a partial joint he had when he saw the car. The clerk didn't know it was Jack's and didn't care. The car was too close to the dumpster and the garbage people wouldn't collect. He called the towing company. It was at the tow yard when it was discovered that the car belonged to Jack, and the owner was missing. By Monday the news had begun carrying stories about the missing father and son.

Sara was grilled by the police. Sara was removed from suspicion because she had a full accounting and witnesses to her actions on that Friday. When she left the motel on Friday, she had gone by Larry's agency to talk with him. Afterwards Sara had gone to Midtown and spent the next five hours having a good time with some college students who were enjoying a weekend home. By the time

Sara went to go get Jack Jr she was nicely buzzed, but not intoxicated. Sara raised the alarm about Jack Jr. The only problem the police had was why she had not tried to contact Jack anytime during the day. Sara answer to the detectives was simple, "I never contacted Jack throughout the day when he was away from the office." This answer combined with the witness statements to her whereabouts satisfied the police.

When Monday rolled around Calvin found himself bored. There was no need to track Jack because Jack was entertaining Jesus. Calvin laid in the bed until 9:30 am when his phone rang. It was the producer from the documentary. To make a long story short, the film company they had hired was incompetent at best. The producer asked Calvin if his company was still available and would like the job at a 20 percent increase from the previous figure they discussed originally. Calvin shot out of bed and said, "Yes Sir! When will the contract be sent over for my signature? Once this is done, we can get started." The producer let Calvin know the contract would be delivered that afternoon via messenger. They wanted to get started the next day because the snafu with the other company was endangering the timeframe they wanted to keep. "Sounds good. I look forward to working with you," Calvin said grinning and ended the call. Calvin was singing *Happy* by Pharrell as he went into the bathroom. Not once did he think about Jack or Jack Jr.

Sara got the money from the movie and after a year of waiting and wondering about her husband and son moved. Sara moved to Austin, Texas where she told friends she could get a new start and put the past behind her.

Calvin only went back one time to the spot where the two Jacks were buried. It was almost two years later. Calvin smiled and dug a shallow hole and placed a DVD copy of the remake of *Riodevous*. The movie was a smash hit and starred several big-name stars. Calvin had stood over the spot and said, "Jack, you did a great job on the script." Calvin used his foot to tamp the dirt back into place then turned and walked back to his truck. A leaf fell onto the spot where Calvin had buried the DVD. The birds and insects continued to play a melody over the spot.

The End
Frank James IV © 2022

ABOUT THE AUTHOR

Frank James IV has been writing in some form or fashion all his life. He enjoys reading, learning, and especially laughing. Check out all his works at: www.thefrankjamesiv.com.

Made in the USA
Columbia, SC
05 February 2025

53340622R00052